Spin My Love

by

Chantal Fernando

All rights reserved. This eBook is licensed for your personal enjoyment only. This eBook is copyright material and must not be copied, reproduced, transferred, distributed, leased, licensed or publicly performed or used in any form without prior written permission of the publisher, as allowed under the terms and conditions under which it was purchased or as strictly permitted by applicable copyright law. Any unauthorized distribution, circulation or use of this text may be a direct infringement of the author's rights, and those responsible may be liable in law accordingly.
Thank you for respecting the work of this author.

CHANTAL FERNANDO
Published June 2014

Cover design © Arijana Karčić, Cover It! Designs
Edited by Lauren McKellar
Proofread by Jenny Sims

SPIN MY LOVE is a work of fiction. All names, characters, places and events portrayed in this book either are from the author's imagination or are used fictitiously. Any similarity to real persons, living or dead, establishments, events, or location is purely coincidental and not intended by the author. Please do not take offence to the content, as it is FICTION.
Trademarks: This book identifies product names and services known to be trademarks, registered trademarks, or service marks of their respective holders, The authors acknowledges the trademarked status in this work of fiction. The publication and use of these trademarks is not authorized, associated with, or sponsored by the trademark owners.
Copyright © 2014 Chantal Fernando
ISBN-13: 978-1499696578

ISBN-10: 1499696574

All rights reserved.

Acknowledgements

Thank you to my sister, **Tenielle**, for your help with this book... Love you infinity.

Thank you to **Ari** for your friendship, wise words and help with anything and everything. I don't know what I would do without you. You really are one of a kind and one of the most amazing people I've ever met in my life.

Thank you to my beta readers: **Kara, Kimberly, Stephanie, Rose and Tash**. You guys! Thank you so much! Most of the time I send you my work last-minute and you always make the time to help me. I appreciate it more than you know.

Rachel Brookes, THANK YOU so very much for your help and for always being there for me. I know you are busy so I appreciate the time you took to give me feedback.

JC Emery, my sprinting buddy! Thanks for your words of encouragement and our daily chats.

Forever Me Romance, you are so much more than a blog to me. You're family. Love and appreciate all the work you do for me. Thank you girls so very much. Rose and Tash I adore you both.

To **all the blogs** that shared my work, or helped promote me in any way—thank you!

And to **my readers**, thank you so much for your support.

Dedication

Tenielle,
My baby sister,
My best friend,
My partner-in-crime,
My hero,
This one is for you.

Prologue

Giselle

The music is pumping but instead of being lost in it, my eyes are on *him:* Tane Miller. This is the first time I've seen him five years.

I'm excited and nervous at the same time. If he really wanted to see me, he would have come home like he'd promised. But he didn't—and I'm here tonight to find out why.

Almost two hours of effort went into my look for the night. I tried to tell myself that it was for me, but I knew that I hoped to impress him. My jet-black hair is ironed straight, teased on top to give it some volume. My fringe slides across my forehead, almost covering one of my smoky, blue eyes. I'm wearing a slinky royal-blue dress, which reaches just above my knees and makes my eyes pop. My tattoos are all fully showcased tonight, the half sleeve down my left arm, and the red bows I have on the back of each of my thighs. The bow tattoos look like they are on black garter belts. It's a sexy look—or so I've been told.

I've changed a lot during the last few years. I've lost weight, my hair is a different colour and style, and I have mastered the art of applying makeup. More than that, more than the tattoos and other physical differences, I feel like a new woman on the inside. I'm more confident, and I know who I am.

At the end of his set, I make my way closer to the DJ booth, hoping to get his attention. I know he recognises me when his pale-green eyes instantly zoom in, oblivious to the other women around me vying for his attention. He's a sexy man. He's dressed in all black, and it looks good on him. His tall build is slightly leaner than I remember, and his dark-brown hair is longer, almost down to his chin.

It suits him.

A lot.

There is something different about him, though. His eyes contain something they didn't all those years ago. They are harder, *colder*.

I don't know what to make of it.

When he heads in my direction, I forget my train of thought. There are a few things I need to say to him—what I came here to tell him. Things I need to get off my chest. I open my mouth to say something to him as he gets closer, but as soon as I'm within reach he pulls me into him, fusing his mouth with mine. He tastes like mint and whiskey, and his lips are firm and demanding. This kiss is different than the ones he gave me all those years ago. I lose all common sense.

This is Tane, after all.

He pulls back and stares into my eyes, his now filled with desire mixed with a hazy look.

"Come with me," he commands, his voice deeper and huskier than I remember. He puts his hand on the small of my back and leads me outside the hotel club. We step into an elevator, but we aren't alone. I'm about to talk to him when his phone rings. He answers it, and I listen to his deep voice, greedily taking in the sound of it. He hangs up the phone as we exit the elevator and walk to his suite. I feel a little nervous. Why hasn't he said anything? The Tane I knew would have bombarded me with questions about Gage and Levi and would have asked how I have been all this time.

But I get nothing from him.

Before I can ask him why, his mouth is on mine once again.

Thoughts forgotten, I close my eyes and feel, savouring the moment. I can't believe I'm here right now. After all the dreaming, hoping, and wanting, Tane is finally in my arms.

Right where he belongs.

He starts to slowly undress me, and I do the same for him. He's a little thinner than I remember, but his body is still strong, lithe. He pushes me down on the bed, mouth still on mine as I hold onto him, wanting and needing him closer.

We make love frantically, roughly. He thrusts into me whilst kissing my neck, my shoulders, my lips, paying attention to every part of me. Afterwards I lay my head on his chest, falling asleep with a small grin on my face.

I'll talk to him when I wake up.

That is my last thought.

*****

I smile when I wake up, feeling sated and satisfied, but then frown when my arm reaches out for Tane to find the other side of the bed cold and empty.

Tane.

I sigh dreamily. I can't believe we finally slept together. I've wanted this moment since I was fifteen. Now, I need to talk to him and hope that I can convince him to come home to visit us every now and again. I don't know why he cut us out of his life, but I intend to find out. He may have distracted me last night, but that wasn't going to happen today. I blush as I remember what we did together.

Sitting up, I stretch lazily and look around.

"Tane?" I call out. I get up and dress in last night's clothes. Glancing around the room, I realize there's no luggage or personal belongings.

The room is empty.

And Tane is gone.

I wait twenty minutes or so, hoping that maybe he went out for breakfast or something, but nothing. He didn't even leave a note. I scoff at my own stupidity. How could he do this to me? Does he not care about me anymore? Has the fame gotten to his head? How can someone change so much? I've known Tane since we were kids.

I do my first ever walk of shame, out of the hotel and to my car.

Tears drip down my cheeks.

I vow never to be so stupid again.

Chapter One

Five years later

Giselle

I walk to my car after a long day at work. I love my job. Some found it odd that I had always aspired to be a librarian, but I couldn't imagine doing anything else. My mother used to take me to the library when I was a little girl, and we would sit in the corner and quietly read book after book together. The fond memories I have of this place remind me of the relationship I used to have with her. We aren't as close these days.

I hum along to the radio on the drive home, looking forward to seeing Parker. I miss him so much whenever I'm at work. I work four days a week, and each day I feel his absence like a hole in my heart.

I pull into the driveway of my unit. It's a two-bedroom, one-bath, and I love it. While it's not luxurious, the rooms are spacious, and it's bright and cheerful. I unlock the door and walk in, following the sound of laughter. My lips pull up into a grin as soon as I see my brother, Gage, tickling Parker mercilessly. Parker's laughter makes my heart melt; it's my most favourite sound in the world.

"Gage, stop harassing my son," I tease, pulling Parker out of Gage's arms and into mine.

"Mama!" Parker squeals with pleasure. I hug my son against my chest, his head on my heart. I lean down and muss my brother's hair fondly.

"I hope he didn't give you too much trouble, Gage," I say to my brother. Gage is two years older than me. He really is a Godsend; he helps look after Parker whenever he can.

"No problem at all. You know I love to spend time with the little squirt," Gage says with a grin. I do know, and I'm so grateful for it.

Gage looks nothing like me, except for his blue eyes. He has brownish hair and two dimples. He is a lot taller than me at about six-foot-one, with a muscular build.

The women love him.

"I'm gonna get going then, sis. Are you gonna be okay?" he asks as he picks up his wallet and keys.

"I'll be fine," I assure him. Gage lives in an apartment with his best friend—a bachelor pad. I'm disgusted by how messy it gets, so I often go over there to clean it.

Gage kisses my temple before walking to the front door. "Come and lock the door, Giselle," he calls out before he departs. I lock the door, putting in the code and my fingerprint for confirmation. The state-of-the-art security system Levi and Gage installed makes me feel safe. I'm not a paranoid person, but I am cautious.

After we're secure, I turn around and stare down at Parker.

"You hungry, baby?" I ask him. He scrunches his nose at me and nods, his black mop of hair tumbling on his face with the motion. "Okay let's go make some dinner," I say, kissing him on the nose.

*****

After dinner, Parker demands that I build tall towers from the blocks so that he can pretend to be a monster ransacking the city. I humour him and enjoy watching him act out the character.

The doorbell rings. "I'll be right back, Mr. Monster."

Parker nods absently, too busy throwing blocks about. I walk to the door and look at the screen to see who it is. Levi, Gage's best friend.

Levi is a great guy. He's laidback and funny as hell, but he's also caring with a heart of gold. He loves Parker and me as if we were family.

"I come bearing gifts," Levi calls out as he walks through the door. He gives me a quick kiss on the cheek in greeting.

"Uncle Levi," Parker calls out excitedly. Parker has started calling Levi *uncle*. Luckily we aren't dating anymore, or that would be kind of awkward. I drag my gaze over Levi Black. His blond hair is styled messily, a chunk of it falling on his forehead. His skin is tanned from the sun, his blue eyes pale and gentle. He's wearing a pair of black shorts, sitting low on his lean hips, and a black singlet top, showcasing his impressive biceps. He has one tattoo, a band around his upper left arm.

We may not ever be together again, but I can still enjoy the view. He looks like he just came here from the beach, which he probably did. He lives to surf and spends most of his spare time riding the waves. He's a free spirit, which is just another thing I love about him.

"What have you brought?" I ask him, wary but also curious. "Please tell me it's not a lizard or something."

He laughs. "Oh, come on, that was one time."

He brought Parker a pet lizard once and I screamed when I opened the box. Safe to say—the lizard went back to the pet store.

"One time too many," I reply with a shudder.

"Well, for Parker I brought some new toys," he says with a grin.

"YAY!" Parker squeals. I roll my eyes and shake my head. Levi grins unrepentantly. I told him to stop wasting his money buying Parker more toys; the kid already has more than enough. Plus, there just isn't enough room in this place. However, Levi loves to spoil him. He and Gage are always buying Parker clothing and toys so that I don't need to. They tend to dress Parker in clothing identical to their own. While I'd never admit it to them, I do think it's adorable.

I know Levi and Gage do this because they want to help as much as possible. I'm a single mother, and they are really the only family I have here. My parents live overseas, so I don't have them to support me; I only have my brother and Levi. They are also Parker's only male role models, since his father isn't in the equation. Even working full-time, I'm only able to just make ends meet. It's tough, but I do what I can. The support that Levi and Gage give me is incredible. I don't know what I'd do without them.

I watch as Levi starts pulling presents out of the very large bag he's carrying.

"What do you say, Parker?" I ask, eyebrows raised.

"Thank you, Uncle Levi," he answers excitedly.

"You're welcome."

I smirk when I see a child-sized surfboard.

"Now, you can learn to surf with me, buddy," Levi tells Parker, handing him the surfboard. He takes the board from Levi's hands and dumps it on the floor. Parker stands on it and starts making wave noises as he pretends to surf. The concentration on his little face makes me smile.

"Surfing?"

"Why not?" Levi asks.

"Perhaps he should learn how to swim first," I tease. Parker does take swimming classes, and has for a while. Levi has also been teaching him at every opportunity.

"He'll get there soon," Levi says with a proud smile before he turns back to his bag of goodies. Next, he pulls out some dinosaur toys. Parker sees them and squeals, ditching his surfboard. He's going through a dinosaur phase.

My heart melts as I watch the two of them interact. We are so lucky to have Levi in our lives. He really is a good man.

"And for Miss Giselle," Levi adds with a grin. My mouth curves into a pleased smile as Levi pulls out two books that I had been dying to read.

"How did you know?" I gape. It's a trilogy, and I've only read the first one. The books have been extremely popular at the library, so I haven't checked them out, because our library only has two sets.

"Last week you spoke about that book for half an hour. Gage told me to pick them up for you," he says as I walk over and give him a small peck on the cheek. "Thank you Levi," I say as I run my hands over the beautiful book covers.

"Anytime, Giselle. Now, I gotta get going. I'll see you tomorrow at our place."

"Okay, thanks again," I tell him. He flashes me a grin and bends down to give Parker a kiss on the head before he takes off.

"Mama! Come and play dinosaurs with me, please," Parker calls out, raising his head for a moment before looking back down at the toys.

I walk over to him and kiss him on his chubby cheek, then get down to business. Folding my legs beneath me, I get down to his level. "I'll be the T-Rex," I say in a silly voice.

*****

It's Saturday, and I'm cleaning up while Parker finishes his lunch. The doorbell rings, and I walk quickly to answer it. Looking through the peephole I see Keira, Levi's sister. She's an interesting character. In her early thirties, she still behaves like an out-of-control twenty-something year old. I open the door with a forced smile.

"Hey Keira." Her blond hair is immaculately curled and her makeup expertly applied. Her boobs are pushed up and on display in a low-cut top, while her legs are covered by skin-tight jeans. Her heels are high enough for me to know I'd probably die in them.

I look down at my ripped jeans and t-shirt with a sigh.

I turn to the little boy standing by her side with a genuine smile. "Good afternoon, Justin," I tell him, giving his blond head a kiss. "Go on in. Parker should be finished with lunch by now." Justin runs past me, slipping his backpack off his tiny shoulder without a word. He rarely speaks, but he is getting better.

I turn to Keira. "Plans for today?" I say, trying to make conversation rather than shut the door in her face.

"Some of us have lives," she responds bitingly. I don't know why I bother. She gives me a little wave with her manicured claws and turns on her heel without another word. I shut the door, closing my eyes, begging for patience.

I can't stand her. I try to, because I love Levi and Justin, but heaven knows I would rather wring her neck than play nice.

When I go back into the kitchen, I see Parker is showing Justin his new dinosaur toys. There are a lot of "oohs" and "ahs". Besides the blond hair, Justin looks nothing like his mother. His eyes are dark and his skin pale.

"All right boys, let's get your backpacks," I tell them.

They cheer as they run to get their bags.

*****

"I did not say that!" I gasp, outraged.

"Yes, you did, sis." Gage laughs. This is the worst part about hanging out with my brother; he loves to bring up embarrassing stories from the past, and trust me, he knows heaps of them. Truth be told, I looked a little different when I was younger. Well, very different. I was plump, okay, chubby, and not too much to look at. While I wasn't really bullied, I definitely wasn't popular. Much the opposite of my older brother.

"I did not follow Tane Miller around!" I deny. I'm lying, because I so did. These stories are the worst, the ones from our youth involving Tane. I hate having his name brought up, over and over again. All of our memories now feel tainted. I place a fake smile on my face, pretending that speaking of him doesn't make me want to punch something. Or someone.

"Giselle, you walked the long way home every day just to spend more time with him," Gage adds, rubbing his hand over his chin. Gage and Levi were obviously aware that I had been infatuated with their friend, but I don't think they ever realised just how deep it went between Tane and me. They all treated me like I was way younger than them. Two years wasn't much—at least, to me—but Tane acted like it was. There was always an emotional connection between us, a cord that tethered us together. We were friends, but I always thought it would turn into more. He had even hinted as much.

"When you turn eighteen …" He trails off, a hint of colour in his cheeks.

"What?" I ask, tilting my head to the side. I was fourteen and sitting on the hood of my parents' car with Tane, just talking, about anything and everything.

"I'll take you to one of those parties you're always begging to come to," he finally says.

I pout. "You and Gage go now! And you're sixteen!"

"Yes," he says patiently. "But we're boys."

I gasp. "That's not fair."

"I never said it was," he replies, grinning.

"You just don't want me to go so I don't see you with Sarah," I grit out.

The smile drops from his face. "Who told you about that?"

"We go to the same school, Tane. What did you think? No one gossips?" I reply, looking away from him.

"You're young, Giselle. You don't need to be talking about these things," he finally says, reaching over and tugging on my hair.

"I got asked out on a date," I announce to annoy him.

"By who?" he growls.

"None of your business," I reply, sliding off the car. "Have fun with Sarah."

He slides off and follows me into the house. "Who, Giselle?"

"Why don't you worry about your own girlfriend?" I snap, feeling hurt. I hate fighting with him, but the double standards need to stop.

"She isn't my girlfriend," he replies, exasperated.

"Then what is she?" I ask, turning and staring at him right in the eyes. I want him to admit it, to my face.

"She's ... someone to keep me occupied until you are old enough."

Both of our mouths drop open. He can't believe he just admitted that, and neither can I.

"I mean ... fuck ... I didn't mean ..."

"You like me," I announce, my lips curling up.

Tane sighs. "You know I do, but you aren't ready, Giselle."

"I will be," I reply. And then I will be all his.

His lip twitches. "Yes, you will. In a few years."

"A few years?" I gape.

"Tane! We're going surfing, are you coming?" my brother asks, walking towards us.

Great timing, Gage.

Tane nods and they walk off together, but not before he throws me one last pleading look.

"Leave her alone, Gage," Levi adds with a chuckle, pulling me back to the present.

"I wonder what ever happened to him," Gage muses. I know he's not referring to his career, which everyone knows about thanks to the media, but why he doesn't ever catch up with his old friends anymore. Why he left without turning back.

"Who cares," I mutter under my breath as I roll the dice, trying to redirect everyone's attention to the game of Snakes and Ladders we were playing with Justin and Parker.

"If only Tane saw Giselle now," Levi says with a sexy half-smile. I inwardly groan. I definitely wasn't about to tell them that he had seen me, and all I was worth to him was a *wham, bam, thank you ma'am*. Hell, he didn't even buy my breakfast. Or talk to me, for that matter. The thought makes me angry. Mostly at myself.

"Giselle is too smart to get involved with someone like Tane," Gage says dismissively. That hurts. I shift uncomfortably, squeezing my eyes shut for a second.

"So where has Keira gone today?" I ask, changing the subject.

"Out," Levi says pointedly. That means Keira has found a new boy, but Levi doesn't want to say in front of Justin, her son.

"I see," I say softly. That explains the cleavage and stripper heels.

"I got a six," Justin announces happily. He's such a good kid. He continuously pushes his sandy-blond hair from his face, revealing those big brown eyes. I should tell Keira to get him a haircut, but I can only imagine how she'd take that.

I watch as Parker slowly moves his counter, thinking no one's watching. "Parker! That's cheating," I say, trying not to laugh. My baby is sneaky. I put on my serious face.

"You said you have to make your own luck, Mama," Parker replies. My eyes widen. Damn kid is already using my own words against me.

"Yes, but when you're playing a game you can't cheat. It's not honourable," I say sagely. Parker thinks it over, then nods.

"Knights don't cheat," he says, biting his bottom lip. He wants to be a knight when he grows up. I don't have the heart to tell him he's a few centuries too late.

"No, they wouldn't," I agree. "So neither should you." He gives me a nod.

"How about we all watch a movie?" I ask the boys. They both nod eagerly, so we put on *Madagascar*, which I know for a fact is Levi's favourite, although he won't admit it. The way his eyes light up when the introduction song comes on confirms it. We all squish together on Gage's soft black couch and watch the movie. I look around, my gaze touching each of the four boys individually. This is my family. Justin and Parker both snuggle into me, and I exhale in contentment.

*****

I pull into Keira's driveway the next evening and park the car. I open Justin's door and let him out. Parker's staying another night with Gage and Levi—they insisted I needed a night to myself. They wanted to keep Justin for another night too, but we were unable to contact Keira.

Keira's house is enormous. It makes mine look like a shed. After her divorce, she got the house and a huge settlement. I'm not sure about the finer details, but I know her and her ex-husband now can't stand the sight of each other. He doesn't come and see Justin at all, just sends money to fulfil his fatherly duties. Like that is supposed to make up for his absence.

The two-storey house is cream coloured, the roof a rustic brown. The porch itself is the size of my living room, with a dainty table and matching chairs that look completely ornamental. The garden is carefully maintained, and the hedges are the straightest I've ever seen. She hires people to do everything for her, of course; nothing is done herself.

I unbuckle Justin and pull him from his booster seat, lifting him into my arms. "Oh, we almost forgot your new toys, Justin," I say as I reach into the car and pull out his bags. Levi spoils his nephew as much as he spoils Parker.

I walk up the familiar path to the double doors, both made of fine wood. I press the bell twice, but after a minute or so there is still no answer. I know Keira is home, because her car is in the driveway along with an unfamiliar black, expensive-looking car. I turn the fancy brass doorknob, to find it unlocked. I glance at my watch; it's ten minutes past seven. I always drop Justin home around seven, so she should be expecting us. I assume she left the door unlocked for me, so I walk in, and head into the living area.

I put Justin down, kissing him on the forehead. "Bye Aunt Giselle," he calls out as he takes the bag from me and heads to his room, no doubt to play with his new toys. I smirk, shaking my head at him. "Keira!" I call out, walking through the lounge room. I hear a noise in the kitchen so I head straight there.

"Oh my God," I yell upon entering the room, bringing my hand up to shield my eyes.

Most people cook in their kitchen. Oh, how I wish she were cooking, because then I wouldn't see her butt-naked, kissing some guy on her kitchen table.

"Keira, your son is home! For fuck's sake," I yell at her, turning around so I don't have to see anymore. I hear her mutter a curse, then shuffling. Hopefully they are getting dressed. The woman is unbelievable! She knew Justin was going to be dropped off today.

"You have a kid?" asks a deep, rumbly voice.

I tense.

That voice.

Surely not ...

I turn around slowly, no longer caring about their nakedness, and look straight into the cold eyes of Tane Miller himself. The man really does get around. My throat burns, and my chest hurts, but I try to school my expression.

Don't let him see how much he hurt you.

He's leaning against the table lazily, without a care in the world, wearing nothing but a pair of boxer shorts. His chest is heaving slightly and I try to push the thought of what the two of them were up to before I arrived aside.

It makes me feel sick.

Tane looks more muscular and filled out than when I last saw him. I stop myself right there, not wanting him to see me staring at him, not wanting to notice how good he looks. Keira is quickly dressing herself, with a sour expression on her face. She walks over to me and says in a hushed tone, "Can you keep him tonight, please? It's Tane Miller!"

I narrow my eyes at her. I want to say no. I don't want her to fuck Tane. But he isn't mine, and I don't get a say in who and what he does.

Clearly he isn't the same person he used to be, and I need to stop forgetting that.

"Yes. But for the record, you're a selfish bitch," I reply loudly. "Have some class, Keira." Okay, so maybe I'm not one to criticise, considering I slept with Tane literally without one word being spoken, but at least I didn't have a child to think about at the time.

I glance at Tane one last time to see his eyes on me, crinkling in thought. He has nothing to say to me? Nothing at all? Fine. Fuck him. I walk out of the kitchen and into Justin's room. I pack his bag, and take him back home with me, pushing away the pain I feel.

Tane doesn't deserve it.

Chapter Two

Tane

I'm leaning against the marble table, staring at the spot that woman just vacated.

It can't be … could it?

It's those eyes.

Giselle.

Hauntingly beautiful, ice-blue eyes.

Keira turns to me with a huff. Her top is on inside out, but I don't bother telling her. I want to get out of here, ASAP.

"Fucking Giselle. She thinks she's so much better than everyone else."

I stand up straight. "Giselle?" I repeat, unable to feign indifference. A bad feeling creeps up my spine. Fuck, it was her. Why did she have to see me like this? And I didn't even speak to her.

Regret fills me.

"Yeah, you were friends with her brother, Gage, weren't you?" she says as she starts to undress again, obviously wanting to get back to business.

She looks so different. My Giselle didn't have any tattoos, her hair was lighter and she was curvier. But those ice blue eyes ...

A memory flashes in my mind, confusing me.

"Fuck!" I curse. I'd only just gotten back in town, and I didn't plan on seeing Giselle so soon. I wasn't ready yet—didn't want her to see what I've become. The man I am now is different from the one she knew. I've pretty much avoided everyone I knew from high school, all my old friends, for the last several years. But now she's already been exposed to this, I can only imagine what she thinks of me. I curse again, and then turn my gaze to Keira.

I've fucked this up so bad.

She's leaning against the wall suggestively, but I ignore it. She was just someone to keep me occupied for the night, no commitment or drama, but that sure as hell isn't happening anymore.

"How do you know her?" I demand.

"Giselle? I'm Levi's older sister. I told you that," she says. She might have told me, but I sure as hell hadn't been listening. Levi Black's sister? Shit. Come to think of it, I had heard rumours about her in high school, and her rep might just be worse than mine. And now she is willing to send her kid away to have sex with me? Because I'm famous? Yes, I heard her comment to Giselle.

It's Tane Miller!

Heaven-fucking-forbid, someone like me for me.

She puts her hand on my chest, and I flinch. I sure as fuck don't want her touching me anymore. I push her away and put my clothes back on, only thinking of Giselle.

Christ. She must be disgusted by me. And she would have every reason to be.

"Where are you going? We're not done," she whines. She tries to pout seductively, but it just looks ridiculous. I ignore her feeble attempts at seduction and concentrate on something else.

Giselle. I need to talk to her, now. I can't leave things like this. Better late than never, right?

"I have somewhere I need to be," I say. I put my shoes on and walk to the door. I pause with my hand on the doorknob. "Where does your brother live these days?"

"He has an apartment in Hale," she says, her fists tightly clenched at her sides, giving away her anger. I'm tempted to ask for the address, but I decide against it. Surely I can figure it out.

When I open the door I feel her hand on my shoulder, stopping me from leaving.

"We're gonna hook up again, right?" she asks, biting her lip.

I wouldn't want to give her false hope, so I just mumble a goodbye and walk out.

*****

Thanks to social media, it wasn't hard to get Gage's phone number. He'd been shocked when I called and that made me feel even worse. Gage and Levi are good people, and we were thick as thieves back in the day. After I left rather suddenly, I turned my back on my old life. I only hope that I can make things right with all of them.

And Giselle.

How I've missed her over the years. I thought about her constantly, but I was too chicken-shit to reach out. Was she married?

The thought is like a punch to the gut.

Besides my mother, I've never cared for any girl as I did for Giselle. She's kind, gentle, and beautiful. At least that's how I remember her. The fit, tattooed woman I'd seen earlier was a stark contrast to the girl I knew, but she's still her.

I knock on the door of apartment number twenty-eight. I run my hand through my hair and take a deep breath. Who knows what kind of reception I will get from Levi. I haven't seen neither him nor Gage in years. We had been best friends and partners in crime since I can remember. But that was before, and this is now. So much has changed since then.

The door opens slowly, and I look up into the blue eyes of Gage Reece. A grin is spread across his face, and he pulls me into a brief, tight hug.

"Tane! Long time, no see, man," he drawls. Gage looks bigger than I remember. Taller, more toned. More intimidating.

"I know. How have you been?" I ask.

"Can't complain," he says with a familiar grin. He waves his arm as an invitation for me to enter, so I do. The place is nice, but it's clear that men live here. There is limited furniture, and pizza boxes litter the kitchen table. Gage opens the fridge and offers me a beer.

"Nah man, I'm fine." He shrugs and grabs two.

Gage leads me into the living area where Levi is lying on the floor on his back, lifting up a little kid in the air with his feet, like a flying airplane. Gage hands Levi a beer when he puts the kid down.

"Uncle Levi!" The little kid laughs gleefully. Uncle Levi? This must be Keira's kid; Giselle must have dropped him off here instead.

"Levi, look who I found," Gage calls out. Levi tickles the kid a few times before looking up.

"Damn, man, when Gage told me you'd called I was in shock," Levi says, standing up so that he could give me a clap on the shoulder. Levi looks a little different; his blond hair is longer, and he too is built bigger. However, his eyes are the same, both gentle and friendly. "Welcome home."

"Ummm ... thanks," I mutter ungracefully. I wasn't expecting this. I don't know why, but I'd expected them to be angry and demand answers. I mean, I had left. I'd never sent them so much as a postcard.

"What brings you back?" Levi asks me. He takes a seat on the couch, so I follow suit and take the seat opposite him. The kid jumps up onto his lap and looks at me curiously, half his face hidden by a mop of black hair.

"I'm taking a six-month break, so I'll be home for a while," I say.

Both of them grin. "Sounds good, man, we can catch up," Gage says.

"You both live here?" I ask them.

"Yep," Levi responds.

"So, what are you guys doing with yourselves these days?" I ask, genuinely curious. I find myself realizing how much I've missed these two. It's not every day you meet friends like them. Hell, I don't have any friends in my life that I can trust like I can Levi and Gage, even after all this time.

"We own and run a security business," Gage says. "Boring compared to you, but it's doing us good."

I laugh. "You'd be surprised. I'm jealous that you get to stay in one place. This break is much needed."

The little boy comes and sits next to me, checking me out. I smile when I notice he's dressed in the same black pyjama pants and white singlet as Gage.

"Hello," I tell him, feeling like shit that I was about to bang his mother earlier. *Again.* Apparently while he was in the house too.

Fuck, I'm a bad person.

"Hi, I'm Parker," he says, extending his hand to me. I take his tiny, chubby hand in mine and shake it.

"I'm Tane. Nice to meet you." I feel awkward. I've never really spent any time with kids but Parker seems like a cool little guy. Gage and Levi must be good to him, because I don't imagine his mother is winning any parenting awards.

When Parker looks up at me, I still. His eyes; pale green. It's like looking into a mirror. For a moment I wonder whether I have slept with Keira before now. Maybe I didn't remember? Surely not; Keira would have mentioned it. It hits me how fucked up it is that I have to question whether I'd slept with someone or not. There have been so many women that I might not even remember.

I'm so messed up.

"So, how are your families?" I ask, trying to be smooth. Two pairs of eyes snap to mine. I guess that didn't come out as I'd hoped

"I'm guessing you mean Giselle," Gage says with his eyebrow raised. "She went home; she was just here."

"How is she these days?" I ask, not bothering to deny it. Gage smiles fondly. He always did have a soft spot for his little sister.

"She's good, man. She works at the library when she's not with Parker." So she must take care of him often, then. No wonder he's such a cool little kid.

"Man, it's been years since I spoke to her," I say. I'm technically not lying. I did say "spoke to" not "saw".

"Well you probably wouldn't recognise her. She's changed a lot over the years," Levi says, rubbing his thumb and index finger over his chin. Gage slaps him on the back of his head. I mentally agree with him. Giselle didn't look anything like I remembered. Hell, I almost didn't recognize her.

"What? She's beautiful," Levi defends himself adamantly, rubbing where Gage had hit. I bite my lip, not liking the way his eyes twinkle when he talks about her.

"She's always been beautiful," I blurt out. I clear my throat and ignore their pointed looks. "Is she married?"

Gage stares me down. "No, she's not married."

Levi gives me a searching look. Am I being that obvious?

"She'll be here tomorrow morning. Where are you staying?" Gage asks, pulling me from my thoughts.

"I've bought a house near the beach," I tell them. I'd considered renting, but I had the money and my financial advisors said a house in Perth would be a decent investment.

"Sweet, man, that's cool," Gage says, nodding.

"Can we play PS4?" Parker interrupts.

"Sure, buddy, what do you wanna play?" Levi asks.

"A shooting game," he says cheerfully.

"You want your mum to kill us?" Gage asks with a chuckle. Somehow I can't imagine Keira caring about whether the games the kid played were child-appropriate.

"I won't tell! I'm no snitch!" Parker insists, his eyes huge on his small face. I can't stop the laugh that escapes me. I can't remember the last time I've laughed. This kid is a riot.

"You gonna stay and play, Tane?"

"Sure," I answer. "Why not."

I'm playing my second game with Parker when I notice Gage staring at me with a weird look on his face. His eyes flicker between Parker and me. I wonder if I've done something wrong. They seem pretty casual around the kid, but maybe I said something inappropriate.

"Everything cool, man?" I ask.

He shakes his head, as if clearing it. "Yep. Prepare to get your ass, ah, I mean butt, kicked."

I smile, game-face on. "Yeah, we'll see."

Parker beats us all.

Once Parker goes to sleep, Gage, Levi and I chill out. It gets late, so Gage tells me to crash in the guest room so I don't have to drive all the way home. I take him up on his offer, feeling too tired to drive.

For the first time in ages, I go to sleep thinking things just might get better for me.

Chapter Three

Giselle

I open the door with my key, pausing to pick my handbag up from the floor. I just finished my kickboxing class. I started doing it after I gave birth to Parker, to lose the extra baby weight, and it had become addictive. I've gone every week since then.

"Parker?" I call out, heading straight to the kitchen. I come to a stop when I take in the scene before me.

Tane Miller is making breakfast. For my son. Two identical pairs of pale-green eyes raise when they see me enter. Parker gives me a huge grin. I force a smile, blinking slowly a few times. This was not something I'd ever thought I'd see: Parker and his father, standing side by side. It's so obvious that Parker is his son; did Gage and Levi notice? I look around the room before my eyes find Tane again. Feeling a little unsure, I take a step closer, wondering how much Tane knows.

"Giselle," Tane says almost reverently.

So now he addresses me. Why not before when we were at Keira's? Did he not recognise me? Maybe he's trying to play that night off like it never happened.

"Tane," I say sharply, in what I supposed was a greeting. I see his forehead wrinkle in confusion, most likely surprised by my dismissiveness. I realise he probably wasn't used to women who didn't fawn over his every movement.

"I'm sorry about yesterday, Giselle, I had no idea that …"

"Don't worry about it, Tane. What you do isn't my business," I say, cutting him off. He thinks I'm upset because I saw him about to have sex with Keira? And while yes, that hurt badly, it's nothing compared to what he's done before. My whole body tenses when I see his gaze trail over the tattoos on my arms, his eyes widening.

Is it possible that he doesn't remember that night between us?

*****

Tane

"Giselle," I say again softly. I love saying her name. She looks beautiful. Now that I have time, I look over her every feature. That jet-black hair is tied up in a messy ponytail. Her face is flushed and her bright, blue eyes are piercing.

"Parker go into your uncle's room for a minute, please," she tells the kid, fussing with one of the bracelets piled on her wrist. I can't help but check out her body. The tight pants and tank top she's wearing hug her every curve. She must have come here from the gym or something.

"Okay," Parker answers, doing just that. I stare at her beautiful inked artwork. Something about the pieces are slightly familiar.

"How have you been? You look so different," I tell her honestly.

"And you haven't changed at all," she says. The tone of her voice is surprisingly harsh. Her words sting.

"I guess it's not just your appearance that's different," I say, eyebrows raised. "You used to be so quiet and sweet." I had meant for it to be a light-hearted comment.

I didn't expect to hear her laugh coldly. "I used to be a lot of things."

She has changed. And it's something more than the weight she's obviously lost, the hair, tattoos and makeup. I can't help but miss the old Giselle. She was something else. Kind to everybody. I was always protective of her. Sweetness like Giselle's needed to be savoured, because it doesn't come along very often. I left before I had a chance to do that.

I rub my chest where it suddenly burns.

"What brings you back home? Slumming it?" she asks as she walks into the kitchen and pulls an apple out of the fridge, slamming the door closed behind her.

"I'm taking a break," I tell her. "Finally visiting home."

"How long before you leave again?" she asks, raising an eyebrow.

"You know why I left last time, Giselle," I tell her. She sighs, her body releasing some of the tension she was obviously trying to hold. She washes her apple, and then takes a small bite out of it.

"Do I?" she replies. "I think it was about more than just losing your mum."

It was, but I don't say anything.

"I'm sorry, but you left a lot of people behind as well, Tane," she says frankly. "It's been years since any of us heard from you." I swallow hard when I see the emotion blazing in her blue eyes.

"Hey sis," Gage greets her as he walks out of the bathroom, a towel wrapped around his waist. I watch as she walks over to her brother and kisses him on the cheek, before disappearing into one of the rooms. Gage gives me a curious look as she walks away, but says nothing.

"You want to head out and catch some waves?" Gage asks me. "I have a spare board." I nod hesitantly, wanting to talk some more with Giselle, but I guess now isn't the time. Some surfing with my old buddy actually sounds good. It's been a while. I linger in the kitchen, waiting for Giselle to come out. When she does, she is hand-in-hand with Parker.

"We're going to get going," she tells us.

"Bye Uncle Gage! Bye Tane!" Parker calls out. I notice Giselle stiffen noticeably.

"Bye little man," Gage says, leaning down and kissing him on the forehead.

"Bye Parker," I say, but my eyes are solely on Giselle.

"Mama, can we get ice cream on the way home?"

My heart skips a beat.

"Sure thing, baby," she replies with a warm smile. I watch them both walk out of the apartment, not looking back.

I stand there, staring where they were in my last view of sight, shocked. Parker is Giselle's kid? Not Keira's? Feeling confused, I remember the colour of his eyes and frown.

Who the fuck is the father?

Chapter Four

Giselle

The week passes slowly so I welcome Friday with open arms. I can't seem to get Tane off my mind. I keep thinking about us growing up. How he had been. I compare my memories of him to his behaviour five years ago, and then recently. Seeing him almost naked, getting down with Keira, had been torture. I couldn't get the images out of my head, and they made me feel nauseous. Yet, despite every ounce of logic telling me that Tane was nothing but bad news, I can't help the feelings I have. I just have to write them off as being the lingering emotions of a young, insecure girl.

That is not who I am now.

*****

Levi told me that Tane has been hanging out with him and Gage, catching up any chance they can get. I have no idea how to process that. Is he going to stick around this time? What do I tell him? It's so embarrassing to admit what happened that night. He's acting as though he doesn't remember. Is that even possible?

Well, this is Tane …

I can't let it go on any longer. He and I need to have a chat.

He deserves to know he has a son.

The library has ten minutes until closing time, so I finish putting away the last of the returned books. Gage told me to come over straight after work for dinner and movies. Parker is already there, since Gage picked him up from kindergarten. Owning their own business, Gage and Levi enjoy a level of flexibility that I could only dream of. They really are a godsend. Without them, I'd have to put Parker in day-care some afternoons. Besides being insanely expensive, I just wouldn't want to do that. It makes me feel much better to know that he is with family.

I finish up and close the library. Heading to my car, I get the absolute shock of my life when I see Tane leaning against it, staring right at me. He's dressed casually in fitted jeans and a t-shirt that gently clings to his toned chest. I can't even deny it. He looks delicious. I've always been attracted to him. I guess that's just something that's never going to change.

"What are you doing here?" I ask him angrily, digging through my handbag for my keys.

"I just wanted to talk to you, alone," he says, his eyes raking over me. I'm dressed professionally in a knee-length black skirt and a white blouse. My hair is pulled back away from my face, pinned in a severe bun, and the only makeup I'm wearing is mascara and baby-pink lipstick.

"How did you know I would be here?" I frown.

"Gage told me you work here. Any more questions?" he asks in a sarcastic tone.

"I don't think you want to go there," I say wryly. I cross my arms, impatiently waiting for him to tell me whatever it is that is so important that it required him to come to my work.

"Look, I'm sorry I left and didn't contact you. But I never forgot you, Giselle. Never," he says, his eyes begging mine. I wanted to hear those words for so long. I wanted him to turn up and reassure me and tell me how much he loved me. But I stopped that after I had Parker. I will not allow myself to be weak because of Tane ever again.

I've already given him so much of me and gotten nothing in return.

"Okay," I respond. Nothing he says will make what he did better. Nothing.

"And I'm sorry about Keira. I had no idea she was Levi's sister, and I sure as hell never expected you to see anything like that," he says, looking down.

"Why? We all know you get around, Tane. It's a bit late to play coy," I tell him sharply, finally finding my keys and pulling them out.

"You're not going to make this easy on me, are you?" he says under his breath.

"Should I?" I ask him.

"Giselle, just ... come here, please?" he begs, as he steps closer to me and pulls me into his arms. I can't help but relax into his body after a moment, closing my eyes and allowing myself to pretend; pretend that this is Tane, my old Tane. Not this new person who has inhabited his body.

"You're beautiful, but I liked you before, too, you know. Just as you were. You've always been perfect to me," he almost whispers into my ear. "I missed you." I pull away. It's all too much.

"Just don't, Tane," I say, raising my hand to stop him from continuing. "Why are you suddenly back?"

"I'm taking a little breather," he says ambiguously. His hands run up my back, causing me to shiver. I take another step back, out of his arm's reach.

"For how long?" I ask him.

"Six months, possibly longer," he replies.

"I see," I drawl.

"So, you have a kid," he says, his tone light, but the sudden stillness in his body gives away his tension.

"I do."

What else am I supposed to say? When I realize Tane is silent, I look up at him, to see him staring at the ground.

"Where is his father?" he asks frankly, his fingers tightening their grip on me. He looks up at me intently, waiting for my answer.

Now it's my turn to stiffen. "Not in the picture." I pull away from his embrace.

"I want a name," he bites out harshly.

"What for?" I ask, now suspicious.

"Because no one hurts you," he says it like a threat.

I can't help the cold laugh that escapes me. "That's rich."

I told myself I was going to tell him; what the hell am I doing? Each comment that comes out of his mouth just infuriates me further.

"What's that supposed to mean?" he demands.

"Nothing. Look, are you coming to Gage's now?" I ask, changing the subject. I will tell him, just not right now. Fuck, I'm scared.

"No, I just left there. I thought I'd let you have some family time," he says, his voice suddenly gentle.

"How kind of you," I say sarcastically.

"What the fuck did I do now?" he asks, looking confused.

"Nothing, Tane. It's Friday, I'm sure you have plans. Keira? Or someone new, maybe?" I say, my fingers digging into my palms at the thought. Instead of answering me, or giving an explanation, Tane just smiles. The bastard smiles. Shit, I need to get a hold of myself.

"I'm going," I announce, pulling myself from his reach.

"I like you being jealous," he says, his lips turned up in a smug grin.

My eyes narrow to slits. "If I was, I'd have to be jealous of how many women around the world? It would be a full-time job."

He shrugs. "I was looking for something, trying to keep myself distracted. What I really wanted the whole time was you."

I open my mouth, and then snap it shut. What does one say to that? He had me. He had me, and he didn't want me.

"You're good, Tane. I'll give you that."

"That wasn't a line, Giselle, give me some credit," he says, looking down at his shoes. "You know there has always been something between us. Connecting us. Drawing us together."

"It doesn't matter. You have no right to say those things," I reply, taking a deep breath, hoping it will calm me down.

It doesn't.

"If we were so connected, you would have come home a long time before now, and I wouldn't have had to run into you by accident. If I didn't walk in on you and Keira, I probably would have never seen you, would I?"

He lifts his face up to look at me. Many emotions pass over it.

Guilt. Regret. Confusion. Love. Loss.

"I never stopped thinking about you, I just *knew* I didn't deserve you," he finally says in a quiet voice. "No other woman will ever have anything on you, Giselle. Never."

I puff out a breath. "That's hard to believe when they get more from you than I ever did."

Now he looks hurt. "What did they get? My body for one night? You got everything else, Giselle. My dreams, my heart. My future. My past. My every fucking thought."

"Your words and actions don't match up. Actions mean much more to me. Now why don't you just go to whoever you will end up with tonight?" I say, regretting the words the moment they leave my mouth.

His face falls. "I'm not seeing anyone tonight. I'm going straight home."

"A bit out of your way, isn't it? Coming to see me?" I ask, knowing it is. The beach is about a twenty-minute drive from here.

Tane shrugs and says, "It was worth it."

I narrow my eyes on him. "What was?"

"Seeing you. I missed your charming personality," he adds sarcastically.

"Ha, ha. I save this charm just for you," I drawl.

"I can see that. Why is that, exactly?" he asks, tilting his head to the side. The motion causes his hair to hide one of his pale-green eyes.

"You're just lucky, I guess," I mumble.

"I'm sorry for leaving you. I'm sorry for the Keira thing. But we weren't together then; you can't really hold that against me."

"We aren't together now either," I point out.

"Not yet," he says as he opens my car door for me.

"Not ever," I say stubbornly under my breath. He ignores it, though I know he heard me.

"I'll follow you to Gage's, make sure you get there safely," he says, his tone commanding no argument.

"That's not necessary, Tane," I say with an eye roll. "Unless one of your groupies comes hunting me down, I think I'll be just fine."

"No arguing, Giselle," he says sternly.

"You just came from there," I argue, pushing away my embarrassment.

The man is being ridiculous right now. I'm so confused. I must have been just another number to him. A number he probably doesn't even remember.

Great. Someone please kill me now.

I hop into the car, and stiffen when Tane leans in to kiss me on the cheek. I pull away from his touch and I see him frown, but he says nothing as he shuts the door. He mimes for me to lock the door, and I do with a frown. Since when does he care so much about my welfare? I mean he used to when we were younger, but this is the new Tane. And the new Tane is a selfish jerk. Right?

At least, that's what I try to tell myself.

*****

Tane

She drives away, and I follow her.

I want her so fucking much.

Little Giselle, the most special girl I have ever met. There has always been something about her. But do I think I'm ready for a commitment?

For Giselle, I could be.

She doesn't have to know about the things I've done, the person I became after I left Perth. I wasn't in a good place then. While Giselle isn't the type to judge, or at least, she wasn't, I still don't want her thinking of me like that. My past needs to stay buried in the past.

When I was at Gage and Levi's earlier, they mentioned a few things about Giselle. The things she's been through, being a single mother. But they said she never complains. She loves Parker unconditionally, just like my mother did me.

I always thought Giselle would be an amazing mother. She's selfless, nurturing, and gentle. She's a beautiful person, inside and out.

And I want her.

I follow her to Gage's and wish I could join her there. Instead, I wait for her to get safely inside and then drive to my beach house. My backyard is literally the ocean. Gage, Levi, and I grew up surfing together and spending every spare minute we could by the beach. I bought this place with that in mind. However, none of us loved surfing more than Levi. He is amazing at it, too; he was asked to compete professionally before I left. I wonder what happened with that.

I park my Land Rover Discovery and jump out, not exactly looking forward to being alone. I like to keep myself busy, keep my mind occupied. It's when I let my mind wander that I think of other things. Of my past. I don't need that shit.

I lock the front door behind me and head straight into the bathroom for a long, steaming-hot shower. Over the years, I've thought about Giselle a lot. Was she happy? What was she doing? Did she miss me? I didn't expect our reunion to be like this. But I don't really know what I expected. I turned my back on my old life, and that included her. I'm a fuck-up, in more ways than one. I've always loved her. We've been in each other's lives since I can remember. All my fond childhood memories have her in them. I always hoped we'd end up together. And I want to make that happen.

I realise that her and Parker are a package deal, and that's okay with me. He's a part of her. I don't know how good of a father figure I could be, but I'd be willing to try.

Do I deserve a chance at happiness?

After I'm dressed in a pair of shorts, I jump into my ridiculously large bed and pick up the book by my nightstand. Books are my new means of escape. They are also something for me to do when I can't sleep, which is happening more often than not. They don't turn me into someone else; they don't hurt anyone I care about.

I turn to the right page and continue where I left off.

Chapter Five

Giselle

I tuck Parker into his bed and kiss him on the forehead. My mind is racing. I have no idea what to think about Tane or the way he was acting towards me tonight, making me believe that he might be interested in me. The thought makes me laugh, and it's not a pleasant sound. After spending the evening with Gage and Levi—who couldn't stop talking about how amazing Tane is, and what the three of them have been up to lately—I can't help but think about him. My mind goes back to the day Tane left. It was the day after his high school graduation.

"Where are you going, Tane?" I ask him, eyeing his backpack and forlorn expression.

"I need to leave, Giselle. I can't be here anymore," he says softly, his eyes roaming over my face as if memorizing it.

"Your mum ..."

"I can't talk about her Giselle. It ... hurts," he whispers, now looking at the ground.

"You can't just leave me … I mean, us," I rectify.

"I'll be back for you, I promise," he says intensely.

"What does that even mean?" I snap. He ignores my question, instead stepping forward and kissing me on my lips. The kiss lingers. I want to push him away, but I can't. Instead I pull him into me and cling on for dear life. He gently removes my hands from the grip they have on his grey jumper, slowly pushing my fingers so they are no longer clenched, then pulls back his mouth.

My fingers touch my lips.

One more longing look.

I love you, he mouths.

And then he leaves.

I open my laptop and type his name into the search engine. I browse a few articles raving about Tane's talent before I check out a few images. I see pictures of him with many different women, also pictures of him out and about in all corners of the globe. He really is into that party lifestyle. One picture of him kissing a stunning blonde has me shutting the laptop closed a little too hard.

It seems like I don't know him anymore at all.

I get up and storm into my room, now fuming mad. He left. He left without caring what happened to me; what happened to anyone. I was in love with him, and he knew it. It doesn't matter that we were young. He can't expect that just because he's back, everything can be as it was before.

It can't.

And he said he'd be back for me.

I guess that was a lie.

*****

I watch as Parker and Justin play together on the playground. I laugh out loud when I see Parker gesture for an adorable little girl to go before him on the slide. Looks like he's going to be a ladies' man.

"I'm going to take credit there for that little move." Levi chuckles next to me.

"Oh? And why is that?" I ask.

"I spent yesterday explaining to him how a gentleman is supposed to treat a lady," he says, looking extremely proud of himself.

"Is that right?" I drawl.

"He's going to respect women," Levi states.

"Of course he is. He's being raised by me," I boast.

"That he is. You ready?" he asks, and I can tell he's impatient by the way he keeps bouncing on his toes. We are taking the boys to the beach, but they wanted to play on the playground first. Levi is eager to get into the water, but he didn't want me to sit here by myself.

"Sure. Parker! Justin!" I call out. Parker snaps his head to me then walks over, grabbing Justin by his arm on the way.

"Let's go swimming. Uncle Levi wants to see what you two can do on your new surfboards," I say, trying to hide my grin. And my nerves. The boys cheer and run around on the sand whilst Levi carries their two boards. Levi is wearing nothing but a pair of low-slung, blue board-shorts. I notice that they are the same colour as his eyes.

"What are you thinking about Giselle?" he asks.

I've been staring.

"Nothing much."

"Hmmmm," he hums, obviously not convinced. I look out onto the water. There are only the slightest of waves, which is why Levi brought us to this beach. He wanted to show Parker and Justin the basics, as well as working on their swimming.

"Tane's been asking about you a lot," Levi suddenly says. Now it's his turn to avoid eye contact.

"And?" I ask.

He clears his throat. "And I think he's interested."

When I'm silent, he turns his face to look at me. "Are you interested in him?"

"Levi …" I start.

"I know, I know. It's not my business," he grumbles, walking towards the water. I put my hand on his arm to stop him.

"You're wrong; it is your business. You've always been there for me. And I know we're blessed to have you in our lives. I don't know what Tane wants, okay?" I tell him. His blue eyes, so much paler than my own, stare directly at me.

I don't know what he wants or how I feel about it. I don't know anything right now.

"Let's teach these boys how to surf, shall we?" he says in a more upbeat tone. I appreciate the subject change more than he could know.

"I don't surf," I say, narrowing my eyes.

Levi gives me a belly laugh. "Don't I know it. Come on, you can swim in the water, and look pretty," he teases.

"Race you to the water!" I say, taking off my t-shirt and running quickly so I get a head-start. I call out to the boys to run with me, and I'm panting by the time I reach the edge. I hear a splash and know that Levi dove straight in. He stays under for an uncomfortable length of time, but I know not to worry. The man lives and breathes the water. He was probably a merman in another life. I take Parker and Justin's hands and walk them in so they are up to their waists.

"Are we going in further?" I ask them, wanting to see if they were going to get their whole bodies wet.

"Yes!" Justin says enthusiastically.

"Ladies first," Parker says with a grin, his pale-green eyes alight with mischief.

*****

The next day, I jump when a finger presses down gently on my back. The book I was holding goes crashing to the floor with a loud thud.

"What does this symbol mean?" comes a masculine voice in a deep baritone, his finger tracing my tattoo. I'm wearing a long-sleeved black off-the-shoulder top with tailored pants, one of my favourite outfits.

"What are you doing here, Tane?" I ask, picking up the book, maybe poking my ass out a little bit more than I need to, before turning around to face him.

"It's a public library. I'm here to read," he says, his grin showing off a dimple in his right cheek.

"Congratulations. The *Dummies* books are that way," I say dryly, pointing across the room. Low blow, I know, but I can't help it that this man makes me want to punch a wall. I resume stacking the books.

"I never pictured you for the Chinese symbol type. It seems a bit cliché; I figured you would get something more original," he says, trying to get a rise out of me.

I sigh, and give in. "I got it with Ciara when we turned eighteen. To celebrate becoming legal. She and I got the same one." Ciara is a friend of mine, another girl we went to school with. She moved away to Scotland last year.

"You still didn't tell me what it means," he says imploringly.

I can feel the heat rise to my cheeks, and I know Tane sees it too, because he starts to laugh.

"Come on, Giselle. It can't be that bad," he encourages.

"Oh you know …" I evade.

"No, I don't," he says, chuckling. "Come on, tell me."

"Dangerous," I say softly.

"What?" he asks. I said it so softly he didn't even hear me.

"Dangerous," I repeat.

"Dangerous?" he says slowly, his eyes crinkling. It's silent for a few moments before he bursts out laughing, earning us a few glares from the library occupants.

"Shhhh! Tane!" I hiss.

"Who gets a Chinese symbol tattooed that says dangerous?" he asks, amusement in his tone.

"Me, obviously," I huff.

"Why?" he asks simply.

"You're a DJ. I'm sure you can figure it out," I say as I pick up a few more books. Tane steps in and starts helping me stack, which is actually sweet. The thought makes me frown.

"Okay, so it must be a song then," he muses.

When he's still thinking after a minute, I blurt out, "Dangerous by Akon."

He laughs again, but this time it's silent. I can still see his body shaking though. Bastard.

"You having fun?" I ask wryly.

"I am, actually," he says. He then starts singing the song, laughing again when he's finished.

"You are nothing like the girl in that song. No one could describe you as a bad girl," he says gently after the laughing subsides. His black hair falls on his forehead, concealing one of his eyes, and I ache to push it back.

"I could have been. You wouldn't know," I snap. *You weren't here.* My resolve against him hardens.

"I doubt it," he says casually, stacking the lasts of the books.

"Don't pretend you know me, Tane." I take in a deep, calming breath, before walking over to my computer and sitting down.

"I do know you, Giselle. Anyway, I was wondering if I could take you and Parker out," he says as he follows me.

I instantly stiffen, and keep my eyes on the screen. "No," I say bluntly.

"And why not?" he asks, not fazed by my attitude.

"Why would I want to?" I counter.

"Because as much as you want to deny it, you like having me around. Besides, I want to spend some time with you. The both of you," he says. The vulnerability in his voice has me glancing up at him.

"Tane …"

"Come on, Giselle," he begs, his eyes pleading with mine.

"Look, Tane," I begin, not quite sure what to say. "I get that you're back in town for a while and want to have your fun or whatever, but please go do it elsewhere."

"What?" Tane asks in shock.

"I'm not an idiot any more. I'm not going to waste time on people who don't deserve it. Parker is my first priority, and …"

"Look," he interrupts. "I know that I hurt you when I left. I know that I should have kept in contact. I know I've been a right jerk. But believe it or not, I've grown up a bit. I'm not eighteen anymore."

I sigh. "I'm sure you have, but you're still a world-class DJ. I'm a librarian with a kid."

He gives me a smile that makes my heart ache. That was the old Tane's smile. "I know. Parker seems great, and I want to spend some time with you. Even if it's just as friends. So please, let me take you guys out."

"I don't think that's a good idea," I say with a sigh.

"Just give it a chance. Afterwards, if you say the word, I'll leave you alone. I promise."

I look into his pleading green eyes and find my defences crumbling.

"Please," he says softly.

"Okay," I tell him. I never could tell him no. It's a weakness. I also think it's time for the truth to come out. I'm being a coward by not telling him. I just know that once it all comes out—shit is going to hit the fan.

The right things aren't always the easiest.

"I'll pick you both up tomorrow night at six."

"Fine."

It's time Tane and I had a chat.

Chapter Six

Giselle

"I guess we aren't going out tonight then," he says quietly as I let him inside, wearing sweatpants and singlet top. I don't miss the way his face drops.

"No we aren't, but I did make us dinner. I thought we could stay in and talk," I say. His expression lightens, and his shoulders relax slightly. I think that he thought I was going to tell him to leave. I open my mouth, but nothing comes out.

"Where's Parker?" he asks me, his gaze darting around my living room.

"Parker is with Levi. Listen, we need to talk about something, okay?" I tell him, gesturing for him to take a seat. He sits, shifting on the seat as he waits for me to talk.

"Hold on I'll pour some wine," I say nervously, clearing my throat before I head to the kitchen, returning shortly with two glasses of red wine.

"I have beer too if you would prefer?" I ask him when he stares at the wine apprehensively.

"Water is fine, Giselle. I'll get it," he says, wandering into the kitchen.

I nod, and start to gulp down my glass, then his glass too.

"You're making me nervous. What do you want to talk about?" he asks when he returns with a glass of water in his hand. He crosses his arms over his chest and studies me intently.

I need to just tell him. Get it over with. Like ripping off a Band-Aid.

I take a huge breath and then begin. "A few years ago you came to Perth to play at The Arena, do you remember?"

"Yes," he says carefully, his eyebrows furrowing.

Here goes nothing.

"I was there that night."

His eyes widen.

"What do you remember about that night?" I ask him.

He looks down and sinks his teeth into his bottom lip.

"It was pretty much like a usual gig," he finally replies. "Sold out event. Afterwards I took a girl back to my hotel room. I remember thinking …"

"Thinking what?" I ask.

Suddenly he stands up. "Fuck, Giselle …"

The look in his eyes can only be described as haunted. "That *was* you that night."

"What do you mean that was me? Do you remember, or are you pretending you don't?" I ask, keeping my tone even.

He rubs the back of his neck nervously.

"We had sex. You bailed the next morning without so much as a word," I say.

"Fuck," he whispers, raw pain etched across his face. I watch as Tane turns his back to me, and buries both of his hands in his hair, pulling on the strands. He suddenly spins and stares at me with an intensity that makes me want to squirm.

*****

Tane

This has to be some sort of sick joke. That was her that night? I remember the night she's talking about. I was fucked up on drugs and I took a girl back to my hotel room. The events are hazy, but we slept together. In the morning I remember looking at her and wondering ... could it be her? She had changed, that's for sure. But when she didn't say anything and left without a word, I thought it sure as hell wasn't her. Giselle wouldn't have done that. She would have stayed, probably chewed me out and called me out on all my shit.

But it *was* her.

And I'm stupid for not realising it.

I can't believe I did this to the one girl in my life that I love. The only one I've ever loved. Who I supposedly care for. What kind of fucked up person am I?

No. I'm not the person I was back then, but that doesn't undo my actions, nor does it absolve my sins. The last time I was in Perth was about five years ago. The thought makes me stand still.

Parker.

I spin around and see the look on her face, on her beautiful face. She has features that would make an angel cry with jealousy. Pink, pouty lips with the deepest Cupid's bow I have ever seen, wide, blue eyes framed in thick, feminine lashes and a button nose. Her chin has a slight dimple in it that I know she hates, but I can't help but find adorable. I want to kiss it. But the look on her face is one I won't be forgetting anytime soon.

It also answers the question that I know is lurking in my eyes right now.

Parker is my son.

I close my eyes as I picture her that night.

Ice-blue eyes.

What the fuck have I done?

"Why didn't you say anything to me?" I ask, my voice a soft whisper. Why didn't she stay? Talk to me? She didn't say a single word. She just acted like all the other girls I've been with. I wince as the thought even crosses my mind.

Giselle is nothing like other girls.

"Well," she says, staring at the floor, "I wanted to talk to you, but first you were on the phone, and then your mouth was on mine and I lost all coherent thought."

I exhale deeply, hating myself in this very moment. "I didn't know it was you, Giselle. Fuck, I'd never do something like that to you; please believe me. Tell me why you didn't say anything?" I ask her again, needing to know this answer.

"I thought you knew," she says in a voice so soft, I have to strain to hear her. "Then I thought maybe you were pretending it didn't happen. I didn't know what to think? Maybe you weren't the same person you were when you left. Maybe you didn't care?"

I walk over to her and pull her into my arms, as close as our bodies can get. Her hair smells like coconut. When I hear her breath hitching I know that she's crying. I rub my hands down her back, not knowing what else to do, or how to fix this.

I had literally just fucked her without a word. Without protection. I've always used protection—at least, every time I can remember. Did she even have an orgasm? Seems like a trivial thing to think of right now, but the fact that I don't even know disgusts me. We stand together in silence, lost in our own thoughts. There is one thing I do remember about the next morning. Why did she leave the room? If she stayed, we could have spoken and cleared all this shit up. It would have still been a shit move on my part, but at least I would have known it was her.

"I'm so fucking sorry, Giselle. Let me make this right," I tell her earnestly. I see the moment she shuts herself off from me. The emotion drains from her eyes as she pulls away, composing herself. "I would never pretend something didn't happen with you, I just didn't know it was you because …"

"Parker …"

"He's mine?" I ask her, already knowing the answer.

She nods.

I'm about to open my mouth to talk to her about Parker when someone rings the bell for the front door. I watch Giselle's back as she leaves to open it.

I'm thinking about everything I have just learnt, coming to terms with the fact that I'm a father when Parker himself walks in behind Giselle.

My son.

My family.

The family I didn't even know I had. And why? Because, like a dumb fuck, I was high and drunk that night. I was fucked up on the night I conceived my son. I feel sick. I never wanted to hurt anyone. I was just weak—lost in my own shit. My own pain.

But enough is enough.

I don't deserve this second chance, but if Giselle lets me, I'm going to take it anyway. I will beg on my knees if I have to.

"Parker," I almost whimper, taking in his features. His eyes are a dead giveaway. How could I have not known? The evidence is staring right back at me. He gives me an odd look, obviously wondering what I'm doing here. Or maybe he senses the tension in the room.

"Go and get changed, Parker. Tane was just leaving," she says to our son. Wait, what? I'm not leaving. I'm never leaving them again, that's for sure. I'm about to say as much when Levi and Gage walk in, both smiling at each other as if they'd just shared some joke. Their smiles drop as they see me standing here, along with the pale look on Giselle's face.

"What's wrong, sis?" Gage asks, instantly alert.

Shit is about to hit the fan.

Levi calls out Giselle's name as he strides over to her. She runs straight into his arms.

It hits me like a blow to the chest.

She whimpers into Levi's shirt, and I take a step forward, wanting to be the one to comfort her. It should be me holding her, not Levi. Yet it's me that caused her pain. I tried to stay away from her for her own good, but I ended up fucking things up anyway.

"Giselle what's going on?" Gage demands, steel in his voice.

"What's wrong?" Levi asks her softly. My fists clench at my sides.

"Tane, what the fuck is going on?" Gage asks again, his posture rigid.

"I'm sorry, Gage," is all she says. What? She's sorry I'm Parker's father? My jaw clenches.

"What happened, Giselle?" Gage demands.

"I'm sorry I never told you. I'm sorry I lied," she says, her voice muffled by Levi's chest.

I swallow hard, before saying, "Parker is my son."

There is a moment of silence.

Of shock.

Then I see the realization dawning on their faces. Levi hugs Giselle closer. Gage stomps towards me, his fist clenched. When he draws it back, I know what to expect.

Pain.

I welcome it.

And then everything goes black.

Chapter Seven

Giselle

I watch in horror as Tane doesn't move to protect himself, he just takes the hit. Gage lifts his fist to hit him again but Tane falls to the ground before he can do so.

"Gage! Stop!" I yell, squirming against Levi's hold.

I hate seeing the two of them fight. They're best friends; time can't change that. I don't want to be the reason that they're fighting right now. I get no satisfaction from it, none.

"Giselle," Levi reprimands as I continue to evade his grip.

"Mama, are you okay?" I see Parker enter the room. I pray he hasn't been there long and didn't see Gage knock Tane out. Levi lets go of me so I can go over to him, squatting down in front of his small body.

"Baby, everything is fine. Go back into your room and I'll come read you a story, okay?" I say, smoothing his hair out of his face. He nods and with a final look at the scene before him, turns around and retreats back to his room.

I lean down over Tane, who seems to be unconscious.

"Gage," I growl, frantically running my hands over Tane's face. I doubt it helps but I do it anyway. Probably more for me, than for Tane.

"So what? He just fucked you and left?" my brother asks, his chest heaving with anger.

"No," I begin, knowing Gage won't like where this goes. "It's complicated. I never told Tane I was pregnant. I only just told him that Parker is his son." I sigh and sit back on my heels, thankful when Tane starts to come to. That's going to be one hell of a black eye, though.

Gage stops. "He didn't know?" He sounds almost hopeful.

"He had no idea, okay? He didn't desert us," I tell him, my eyes pleading. I don't want to ruin their friendship over this, and the problems between Tane and I are just that: only between us. No matter what issues I have with Tane, I don't want Gage or Levi to be mad at him. He doesn't deserve anyone's wrath except mine.

"How could you not tell him, Giselle?" he asks, running a hand through his hair in frustration. "That doesn't sound like something you would do."

I hate the disappointment in his tone.

"We spent one night together, Gage," I say, avoiding going into details. No brother wants to hear about his sister having a one-night stand. "He didn't even recognise me. Look, it doesn't matter, it happened. But he's here now, and we're trying to work out what the best thing for Parker would be. I can't keep him away; Parker would hate me and Tane would hate me."

And my heart might get broken, again. But now it's time to think about Parker, not me. It's all about my little boy.

Gage just stares at me, looking like he wants to hit something else. I look over at Levi, who has an unreadable expression on his face.

"I'm sorry I never told you the truth," I say softly. Levi stares at the ground, not saying anything. "Both of you."

Gage sighs, closing his eyes, as if when he opens them everything will be solved. "He's my friend. But you're my sister, Giselle, and he should have been there for you. I know I don't know the whole story, but you shouldn't have had to deal with this alone."

"Let me handle this, Gage," I plead. He goes to argue, but I cut him off. "No. Just stop. Don't ask me questions when I haven't even figured out how to handle this situation yet. Let me deal with this and I'll explain everything later. For now, I need to think and talk to Tane." I can see Gage thinking it over and when he sighs I know he's agreed.

"We will talk about this tomorrow," he demands, his tone brokering no argument.

"Why did you guys come back so soon, anyway?" I ask him.

"We forgot Parker's bag," he replies. "We didn't know ..." Something like this would be happening? No, I guess not.

I nod quickly and watch as they both leave.

Levi didn't say a word.

I've really fucked up.

Tane opens his eyes, blinking furiously.

"Are you okay?" I ask. It's a well-known fact that Gage is a good fighter and he's built like a brick-house, so I can only imagine how hard he hit Tane.

I watch as Tane shakes his head no, but I don't think it's the pain from the hit that he is referring to.

"Wait a sec," I tell him, getting up and running to Parker's room to check on him. He's lying on his bed, fast asleep, clutching a book. The sight makes me feel guilty. I carefully pull the book from his grasp and put it away, then cover him with his blanket. I kiss him on his forehead and run my hand through his hair. He is such a good kid. I really am blessed.

When I return to Tane, he is sitting on the couch, staring at the wall. I see him staring at the bottle of wine, but not reaching to pour any.

"Why didn't you tell me?" he says, still staring at the wall. I sit down next to him.

"When I found out I was pregnant I tried to ring you. Your publicist answered and refused to put the call through. When I tried to explain to her, she laughed and hung up. I'm guessing she was used to receiving pleading calls from women," I add dryly before continuing. "I decided to fly out to Sydney to talk to you in person. I knew you were doing a gig at a club there, so I went. When I got there, I couldn't find you. Apparently you had left early with …" I trail off, not wanting to go on. I was told he had left with more than one woman, so I just left. I was angry with him. I was hurt. Looking back, I should have just found him. Whether he was busy with other women or not, I should have just looked for him and tried to tell him. He deserved that much. He fucked up, but so did I. I flew back to Perth the next flight.

When Tane lowers his head into his hands with a strangled sound, I assume he remembers the night himself. When he looks up at me, his crestfallen expression makes my heart ache. He shakes his head.

"Fuck!" he growls, standing up and walking out of the house. I walk out behind to see him leaning against his car window, hands crossed against the top of the vehicle. When I see his shoulders slightly lifting, I wonder if he's crying. I walk over to him and place my hand on his shoulder, frowning when he flinches at my touch.

"How can you even want to be near me right now?" he asks, the hollowness of his tone worrying me. I don't understand.

"What do you mean?" I ask.

"All this time you've been taking care of Parker by yourself, while I've been …" He trails off and I try my best not to finish that sentence. I don't want to think about it. No matter what Tane has done, I don't like to see him upset or hurt. He's my weakness.

"It's the past, okay? Now we just need to decide how to handle the future," I say gently. Tane straightens and faces me. His eyes are faintly red, the only indication that he was upset. "I just want you to know that I got into this without expecting any help. I understand that this has been thrown at you and if you don't want to be—"

"I want to be involved, Giselle," he says, cutting me off. The way he says it is almost a question. "Can I come over tomorrow and talk to him?" He clears his throat. "I know I've fucked up, I mean, messed up, but more than anything I want to be in his life."

I bite my lip when he changes the curse word. Maybe he will take this seriously.

"Alright," I find myself saying. "We'll sort this out." He nods, but says nothing.

"Do you want to eat before you go?" I ask him, remembering the dinner I cooked. "And I'll give you an ice pack for your face."

"No thanks, I'm not hungry. And my face is fine," he says idly. "Giselle, thank you."

"For what?" I ask.

His voice comes out as a whisper. "For not hating me."

I could never hate him. I don't know if it's a good thing or a bad thing.

I puff out a deep breath. "I don't hate you. This is a mess, but I don't hate you. We have a lot to talk about, though."

"You're so strong," he says, voice hoarse. "I'll come around tomorrow."

"Okay," I reply.

I kiss him on the cheek and head inside, locking the door and turning on the alarm behind me. When the door is closed I lean back against it, closing my eyes.

What a day.

Things can only get better from here, right?

I knock on wood, just to be safe.

*****

Tane

I bury my head deeper into the pillow, wishing it would swallow me whole. I cannot believe this shit. I've fucked up numerous times in the past, but this really takes the cake.

My actions are now affecting others, affecting my son.

Parker.

Is it possible to love a kid so much? A kid you have only seen a couple of times, and only just found out was yours?

I already knew he was special. I already cared about him because he was a part of Giselle. But now … I don't think words could fully express how I'm feeling. Soul-deep, mind-numbing love.

I have a son with the most amazing woman I have ever met. Even better, she's giving me a chance, despite what a fuck-up I've proven myself to be. I can only hope that she will forgive me, even though I know I don't deserve it. I will be better for them: my family. I sure as hell have a lot of making up to do.

I flip over onto my back and stare up at the ceiling. I wish my mother were here to meet her grandchild. She would have loved Parker, just as she loved me. I run my hand over my face, wincing at the pain around my swollen eye.

I deserved that. I welcomed the pain. Physical pain is easier to take than emotional. Scars heal easier on the outside.

I close my eyes and will myself to sleep. Tomorrow I need to make everything right.

Tomorrow I become a father.

Chapter Eight

Giselle

After a rough night of tossing and turning, I stand barefoot in my kitchen flipping pancakes.

"Pancakes," Parker cheers as he sits down at the table.

"Are your yes-sirs having breakfast with us?" I ask with a raised eyebrow. He has a bunch of toy soldiers in his hand, which he refers to as *yes sirs*. He has called them that ever since he could talk, and I find it too adorable to correct him.

Parker gives me a lopsided smile. "You're silly, Mama."

I grin as I crack an egg to fry in a separate pan. I'm not in the mood for pancakes today.

I serve our food and sit adjacent to Parker. We have breakfast together, and Parker manages to eat most of his by himself. Of course, a lot of the food ends up on the table and floor, and as I'm cleaning up there is a knock at the door. I was wondering when he would arrive.

The walk to the front door seems unusually long.

"Good morning," I say as I open the door wide, welcoming Tane inside.

"Hey," he rumbles. He looks like he didn't get much sleep either. His eye looks bruised and painful. He walks into the kitchen and comes to a standstill when he sees Parker. He drums his fingers on his thigh, clearly not sure how to handle the situation. I watch as his gaze rakes over his son, taking in every little feature. He swallows, and then glances at me for guidance.

"Parker, Tane is here," I say, trying to keep my voice as unaffected as possible. Parker turns around and gives Tane a smile. Tane gives him a forced smile back, his eyes not straying from Parker's face. I have no idea how he wants to do this. Does he want me to tell Parker? Pale-green eyes disappear as Tane squeezes his lids shut. The air in the room is thick.

I clear my throat.

"Tane …"

"Let me talk to him, please," he says in a hoarse voice. His eyes flutter open and the look in them is intense. Pleading. I don't want him to. I feel nervous, not sure whether I should speak to Parker instead. However, I nod, and head back to the sink to finish washing up. I need to give Tane this chance, don't I? He's the one who needs to build a relationship with Parker.

I always defended my actions by saying that I tried, but the truth is I could have tried harder. Tane not having been a part of Parker's life isn't *all* his fault. In fact, I'd say it's mostly mine. It wasn't fair of me to assume that Tane wasn't ready when I really had no idea how he'd have handled the situation if he'd known I was pregnant. This whole situation is a complete mess of *what ifs*. This is the reality of it though, and there is no point in questioning it anymore. It is what it is and we need to make the most of it for my son's happiness.

Tane and Parker walk into the lounge room, side by side. Parker looks up at him, then copies the way Tane pulls at the bottom of his t-shirt. I sigh heavily. I have no idea what Tane's going to tell my son; I just hope Parker doesn't get too upset. I have no idea how he's going to take this, or how much of it he's going to understand completely.

I last a whole minute before I change my mind about being in that room with them.

Screw this.

I turn the tap off and quickly dry my hands on the closest hand towel. I know Tane wants to do this alone, but I *need* to be there. This should be a family discussion.

I walk into the lounge room. Their conversation ceases at my entrance, so I take a seat opposite them and nod at Tane for him to continue. He watches me a moment, giving me a gentle look, then turns back to Parker.

"I know you've only met me a few times, but I'm going to be spending a lot of time with you from now on …" Tane says, swallowing. "I hope you don't mind me spending time here?"

Parker shakes his head. "I like it. You're fun."

Tane grins a little at that. "I'm glad you think so. I think you're fun too."

"I like beating you at shooting games," Parker adds, then turns to me with a guilty look on his face. My eyes narrow on Tane, who shrugs as if he has no idea what Parker is talking about.

Typical.

"Do you know what a dad is, Parker?"

Parker nods enthusiastically. "Bobby has a dad."

I bite my lip to stop it from quivering. Bobby is his best friend, and he likes to talk about him a lot. Everything is Bobby this and Bobby that, but I haven't heard him talk about dads before. We've never really discussed it, other than when I told him that his dad lives somewhere else. He didn't ask why, just nodded and accepted it.

"Lots of my friends have dads, but I don't. Mum said my dad lives somewhere else. Instead I have Uncle Gage and Uncle Levi."

That comment slices my chest open. I don't want to look at Tane's face, but I do. He looks pained. Guilt and regret flash in his eyes. He looks down and then back to Parker's face.

"Would you like to have a dad?" Tane finally asks, his eyes intense.

Parker pauses, thinking, before nodding. "Yes, I think so. Uncle Gage and Levi do lots of dad things with me, but it would be cool to have a dad live with me, like Bobby Pritchett's does."

Ah, crap. I wait and see what Tane says next.

"What about a dad that doesn't live with you?" Tane implores, "but will still be there for you and will see you all the time."

"I guess that would be okay, too," Parker replies, shrugging his small shoulders.

"Well that's good. Parker … because I'm your dad," he says, his voice croaking. "I know I haven't been here. But I will be from now on."

Parker scrunches his nose, tilting his head to the side as he looks Tane up and down. I wonder what is going through his mind right now. I hold my breath as I wait for his response.

"How do you know that you're my dad?" he asks, a dubious look on his face.

My lip twitches at his reaction, and I exhale slowly.

"Well, for one, we have the same eyes."

Parker instantly gets up on the couch and leans forward, getting right in Tane's face. He stares intently into Tane's eyes.

"Hmm, yep, we do," he agrees. "Where were you? Mum said you lived far away,"

Tane swallows. "Yes, I lived far away. It was my fault that I wasn't here, but I hope you will let me make it up to you."

We both stare at our son, waiting to see what he will say next.

Parker thinks it over. "Will you stay this time?"

My breath hitches. My darling boy.

Tane gently puts his hand on Parker's shoulder. "Yes, I will. If you want me to."

"Okay, you can be my dad," Parker decides.

I watch as Tane smiles slowly, his eyes glassy. He exhales deeply, then scrubs his hand over his face. "Thank you."

I realise tears are sliding down my face, and I wipe them away quickly, averting my gaze. Parker notices anyway. "Mum, why are you crying?"

"I'm just happy," I tell him, kissing him on his smooth cheek. He nods, accepting my response, and then turns his body to Tane.

"Want to play with me?" Parker asks, either ignoring or not noticing the tension in the room.

"Okay," Tane says. He turns to me. "Can I spend the day with you guys?" he asks hopefully, his eyes pleading with mine.

I nod, my voice cracking. "Sure."

*****

"He's amazing, Giselle," Tane says, shaking his head in admiration. Our first 'family' day out had been a success. We spent the day at the local indoor play centre. I'd been shocked when Tane actually got on the equipment with Parker to play with him. Watching them together melted my heart. Tane did so well with Parker, and I could tell Parker already adored him.

Parker had been dozing off on the way home, tired from his antics, so he was now in his bed, napping. I'm starting to cook dinner, chopping onions, while Tane sits on the stool opposite my bench.

"I know," I reply with a wink, grinning proudly.

Tane smiles. "I'm serious. He's smart and well-mannered, but he's quick and sneaky too."

I smile in return but say nothing. It saddens me that Tane missed so much, but knowing how much he's enjoying getting to know Parker makes me happy that they have the opportunity to make up for lost time. Better now than never.

"I had fun today," he continues.

"So did I. And I know Parker did too," I say softly. "Would you like a drink?"

"Sure," he says, watching me as I open the fridge and pull out some orange juice. "You remembered," he smiles. He loves his orange juice.

"It's hard not to. You used to drink this stuff by the litre." I pour us some and slide a glass over to him.

"Thanks," he says, sipping on it. His gaze stays on me.

"What?" I ask him, knowing he wants to ask me something.

"When can I see the two of you again?"

I hadn't really thought of this, to be honest. "Parker goes to kindy three half days a week."

Tane sits up straighter. "How would you feel about me taking him on the days he doesn't have kindy? Or picking him up from kindy?"

I clear my throat. "How about you take a week or two for him to get used to you a little more and then we can talk about it?"

He nods eagerly. "That sounds great." I'm relieved that he isn't offended by my hesitation.

"Good," I say. "If it all works out then I'll tell Gage that he doesn't need to pick him up on those days, but for now I think we should take it slow."

His pale-green eyes close. "Thanks for giving me this chance, Giselle."

I sigh. "I was in the wrong too for keeping him from you. Yes, I tried to contact you, but I could have tried harder. I shouldn't have assumed that you wouldn't want to be involved in Parker's life."

He shakes his head. "I wasn't a good person then, but I'm trying to be one now." He glances towards the hall where Parker's room is. "I want to be the father he deserves." With that, he stands and walks over to the sink to wash his glass. "Can we talk about something?"

"About what?" I ask wearily.

"Money," he says, crossing his arms over his chest and staring at me.

"What about money?" I ask, tilting my head in confusion.

He nibbles on his bottom lip. "I haven't given you any money for Parker for the last four years. I want to set up an account for him."

"Um, okay," I say. If he wants to do that, he can go ahead.

"And for you," he adds.

My body stills. "What do you mean, and for me?"

"I want to help you out. I have four years to catch up on."

I shake my head dismissively. "I'm perfectly comfortable, Tane. I appreciate the thought though."

He sighs, rubbing his forehead. "How did I know you would be stubborn about this?"

"Because you're not stupid?"

"You did everything for him by yourself. You worked to support him …"

"Yeah, and?" I interrupt.

"And you shouldn't have had to!" he growls, losing his composure. His chest heaves as he tries to gain control. "It should have been me taking care of both of you."

"Let's compromise. You open an account for Parker. That's a good idea for his future, but you don't need to open one for me, Tane. You have no reason to give me your money. Furthermore, I don't need it."

"Fine," he says, putting his hands up. He doesn't look too happy about it, but too damn bad. I don't want or need his money, and he shouldn't feel guilty. He didn't know about Parker, and like he said, the timing wasn't right back then anyway. In this instance, it looks like everything has turned out the way it should have.

"Can we talk about us?" he asks quietly, leaning his hip against the countertop.

"There is no 'us', Tane," I say, narrowing my eyes on him. "We're childhood friends turned co-parents."

He's silent for a few moments. "You came with me back to the hotel that night. You wanted me."

My mouth falls open. I can't believe he is throwing that in my face. If he wants to talk about that night—then fine. "It was five years ago. I did want you. As in, past tense."

He flinches. "Giselle …"

"We're friends, Tane," I say. "Sure, at one point it looked like we were going to be more. You gave me my first kiss …"

"I remember," he says, a faraway look in his eyes.

"And you said you would be back for me when you left. But you didn't come back. You told me you loved me—"

"I've always loved you," he cuts in.

"But now all we can be is friends."

There is no way my heart is willing to be anything other than friends with this man. I put myself out there for him and look what happened. I don't regret having Parker, not in the least, but that doesn't mean my heart wasn't broken in the process. Not just that, but I used to be a dreamer. I used to look up to Tane, think the world of him. I used to think there was something special between us, something magical.

A love that is usually only found in fairy tales.

Now I know, it was just the musing of a young and foolish girl. It wasn't reality. Tane wasn't my hero, and I wasn't his princess. In fact, he didn't even know it was me when we made love. Or should I say, when we fucked.

It was making love for me, but I guess it was just mindless fucking for him. After all, he had thought I was a stranger. An easy lay.

"What's going on in that mind of yours?" he asks, pulling me from my thoughts.

"Just thinking about that night," I reply on a sigh.

"What about it?" he asks.

"Never mind."

"Giselle," he says shortly.

"I was just thinking about how I thought it was the best night of my life, making love to you, but you didn't even know it was me. You thought you were fucking some random chick," I say, unable to keep the bite out of my tone. Part of me feels embarrassed for being so open, but the rest of me wants him to know how he made me feel.

He covers his face with his hands and makes a pained sound. "You weren't some random chick to me."

"You didn't even recognize me," I snap, hiding my expression behind my curtain of hair. He walks over to me and pushes my hair out of my face. I flinch as his fingers almost graze my cheek.

"You could never be some random woman to me. I'm so fucking sorry about that night, Giselle," he says, burying his face in my neck.

"How could you not know it was me?" I ask in a small, broken voice.

Silence.

"Tane?" I prompt.

"I wasn't in a good place back then," he says.

What does that even mean?

"I don't understand …"

"I used to … have an issue with substances," he says, cringing. "That night, I'd been drinking and I was high."

"Drugs?" I ask, dragging the word out.

Tane was taking drugs? No fucking way, not my Tane.

"No," I whisper. "What the fuck, Tane?"

"I know," he replies, sounding ashamed.

I step away from him. "You were on drugs?"

Is that why he had sex with me?

He nods, and I have no idea what to say. My mind works, all the puzzle pieces fitting together. The way he looked back then, his words of not being a good person or being in a good place.

"Please don't take him away from me," he says, looking down at the floor.

I look around the kitchen. "Are you still using?"

He shakes his head and looks at me, letting me know he's telling the truth. "I haven't been on anything in a year. I swear. I'm done with that part of my life."

"How did you stop?" I ask him. I know nothing much about drugs, except the basics. I can't even imagine what he went through.

"I went to rehab. I'm completely clean now," he replies in a low tone.

"Good," I tell him, not knowing what else to say. "That's … good." The silence between us becomes tangible, the air in the room almost suffocating.

"I need to tell you something about that night though. If you would just—"

"I don't want to talk about that night anymore," I say, cutting him off. It hurts too damn much.

"Okay. I should go," he says. He takes a step closer to me, maybe wanting to kiss me bye, but thinks better of it and walks to the door. There, he pauses. "Can I check on Parker before I go?"

I nod and wait for him as he disappears into his son's room. He comes out and studies me for a few moments before saying, "Lock the door."

I roll my eyes. "I will."

"Can I come see you tomorrow?" he asks, voice hopeful.

"Yeah, okay," I reply, shrugging my shoulders. This isn't going away. Our issues aren't going anywhere. We need to solve them, to make them better, but right now I'm feeling drained.

He says bye once more and then leaves. I lock the door behind him.

It's only later that I replay his words in my head. He wanted to come and see me tomorrow? I'm sure he meant to say Parker.

Because there is no other reason for him to come by.

Chapter Nine

Tane

I glance down at Parker and watch him as he draws a picture. It's more of a scribble really, but regardless I'll be sticking it on my fridge with the other pictures he's drawn me. A week has passed since I found out about him; a week since my life turned upside down.

It's been one of the best weeks of my life.

Giselle has been keeping her distance. She has been kind, even though I know that sharing Parker must be hurting her. This messed up situation we're in; it's really shown me just how amazing she is. There are so many other ways this could have turned out. She could have punished me for how I treated her, but she's not like that.

You don't deserve her. I push the thought away and take a seat next to Parker.

"That picture is amazing," I say as I take out a sheet of paper to join him. Parker grins at my compliment then continues to draw. Today is the first day that he's come to my house to spend time with me. Rather than go to Giselle's place, as I usually do, she said it was okay for him to spend the day at mine.

"I'm hungry," he announces, turning his head and staring at me with wide eyes. There is nothing more refreshing than the honesty of a child. I wish all people were that upfront.

"Come on then, buddy, I'll make you a snack. Your mum said she'll bring us dinner on her way home from work," I tell him, standing up and heading into the kitchen. He follows behind me. I turn and lift him up onto the chair, kissing the top of his head before I walk away. I pull out some celery, carrots, cheese, and crackers, and put them on the table, then start to cut up the vegetables.

"I don't like celery," Parker says, sticking his tongue out.

"This is what your mum told me to give you," I reply, frowning a little. Maybe I heard wrong?

"Mum makes me eat it," he grumbles, his little face falling. He really is too damn cute. I don't know how anyone says no to him at all.

I grin at him. "Maybe you can just eat the carrots instead."

He grins back at me. "Okay."

"I'll eat the celery," I tell him with a wink. I love playing co-conspirator.

"Good," Parker replies, nodding his head sagely. "It'll make you big and strong. That's what Mama says."

I chuckle at the seriousness of his tone. Fuck, I love this little boy. He looks so small next to me. I bought him a bed and turned the bedroom next to mine into something similar to what I had when I was a child, with blue walls and a racetrack on the floor. It took hours to finish it all, but his squeal of excitement when he saw it makes all the effort worthwhile.

Now I just need to make it so I deserve him.

And his mother.

*****

I ignore Gage's unhappy look and walk past him into the apartment. I see Levi sitting on the couch, sipping on a beer and watching the footy. He narrows his eyes on me when he sees me, his lips tightening. They both aren't happy, that's for damn sure.

"Can we talk?" I ask, taking a seat opposite Levi.

There are a few moments of uncomfortable silence as I gather my thoughts. They stare at me expectantly.

"I slept with her that one night, and I didn't even realize it was her," I say, knowing how stupid it sounds to even my own ears.

"Are you fucking kidding me? How could you not know?" Gage growls, crossing his arms over his wide chest.

"She looks so different! And I was high that night," I say, cringing at the word *high*. Hopefully they will assume I was just smoking weed, when really it was a little more serious than that. "She never said anything, never spoke to me ..." I trail off. I don't want to make her sound bad, going to bed with a man without even saying one word. She'd assumed that I knew it was her. I might not have known it was her, but looking back now, I felt it.

I felt something.

After so long, I actually felt something.

She wasn't just another one-night stand. She left *me* that morning.

Gage and Levi share a look. "She never told us who the father was. She never wanted to speak about it, and I eventually dropped it. I mean, looking at it now, it's pretty fucking obvious he's your son. But we never knew you two had seen each other again. Hell, you'd all but fallen off the face of the earth."

"I wouldn't have let her go through this alone if I had known."

"She wasn't alone," Levi snaps, his brows furrowing.

"Right, of course," I amend. I know they have both done a lot for Parker and Giselle. I just wish it had been me doing all those things. Now that I'm here, it *will* be me doing those things, and I look forward to it.

Gage sighs. "I always wanted to hurt the man that deserted Giselle. I just never thought it would turn out to be one of my best friends. And the man Giselle has loved ever since I can remember."

I draw in a sharp breath, feeling like someone had punched me. Yep, that comment hit its mark.

"Are you sticking around?" he asks, studying me.

I slowly nod, then take in a deep breath. "I'll have to go back to work eventually, but yes, I'm not leaving them again."

"Good," he replies sharply, nodding his head.

"Is that it?" I ask, wondering when the punches are going to commence.

Gage studies me. "You hurt her once; I don't think you're stupid enough to do it twice."

"And if you are, we will be there to kick your ass and pick up the pieces again," Levi adds, looking a lot less composed than Gage.

He wants her. Or has he already had her? The thought makes my throat burn, even though I know I don't have a right to feel that way. I don't have any rights, really; not until I make amends and prove myself.

I rub the back of my neck. "I need this second chance with them. I'm not going to take it for granted, I can promise you that."

Gage nods once. "Alright. Want a beer?"

And just like that the air in the room lightens.

"No thanks, but I'll grab a water," I say, getting up and walking to their fridge. I pull out a bottle then go and sit back down. I don't drink anymore, but I try not to draw attention to the fact. It just leads to more questions that I'd rather not answer.

It's not long before Levi gets restless. "Want to go surf?"

We all stand up and head to the beach.

Chapter Ten

Giselle

As I'm getting ready for my gym session, I hear my ringtone go off.

"Hello," I say, answering my phone.

"I'm not dropping Justin off this week," Keira says, not bothering with a *hello*.

"Why not?" I ask. I know Justin loves spending his Saturdays with Gage, Levi, Parker, and myself.

"Well, I heard that you're having drama with your baby-daddy, and I just don't want Justin around that negativity," she says cattily. Baby-daddy? Is she fucking kidding me?

"So, what you really mean is you're pissed that Tane didn't return to you for seconds?"

Silence.

"If I wanted to sleep with him again, I would have," Keira responded. "I just didn't want to after you rudely interrupted us." The beeping on the line indicates she hung up on me.

I shouldn't be surprised that she could be so selfish and petty, but she shouldn't pull Justin away from the people he loves, the people who love him, just because she's a psycho. We're the only stability he has.

I put my phone back into my gym bag and walk over to the equipment. I punch the boxing bag, working my aggression out and pretending the bag is Keira's face. Four more jabs, then I start on my kicks.

"I guess this probably isn't the best time to ask you out on a date, then?" comes a voice from behind me. I turn and face my kickboxing instructor, Greg.

"Really?" I ask, blinking in surprise. I'm sweaty and disgusting right now, red-faced with no make-up, and my hair sticking out in every direction.

Greg smiles. He's good looking, but he knows it, which kind of puts me off. He works out a lot, and I've seen him around the gym flirting with different women. He's not my type.

Still, I find myself feeling a little flattered, especially since I kind of look like shit right now.

"Why not?" he asks, tilting his head to the side. His eyes peruse my body in a suggestive way, and I clear my throat. Yeah, no thanks.

"Sorry, I'm kind of seeing someone right now," I straight-out lie. I offer him an apologetic smile, grab my towel, and head home.

After a long shower, I clean the house then pick up Parker from kindy. Tane calls and asks if he can drop in to see Parker. I tell him yes, because what else am I supposed to say? Parker is his son, and it would be selfish of me to keep them apart.

I just hope he becomes a good role model for my son. My biggest fear is that he'll suddenly decide he no longer wants to play dad, and then Parker is left wondering why he was abandoned and what he did wrong. I can tell Parker loves Tane already. I don't want Tane to disappoint him. I want him to become a permanent fixture in Parker's life.

Right on time at six pm, Tane arrives.

"Hey," I say as I open the door for him. He's wearing worn jeans and a red t-shirt that fits him to perfection.

"Something smells good," he says, stepping inside and closing the door. "Thanks for letting me drop by."

I swallow. "No problem. Parker was asking about you today, anyway."

"He was?" Tane asks, sounding surprised.

I bob my head. "He was. He's in the living room, playing with his toys."

Tane nods and follows behind me. I stop in the doorway and watch Parker as he plays with his toy soldiers. "Do you want to play with him while I finish up dinner?"

"I'd love that," he replies in a low tone. I nod, force a smile and head back into the kitchen. As I set out the food on the dining table, I can hear their laughter from the living room.

I smile, letting them enjoy their time together for a little while longer before I call them for dinner. After I do, Tane walks into the kitchen with Parker on his shoulders.

"Mum!" Parker calls out, a huge smile plastered on his face. "Look at me."

"I can see." I giggle. "Come and eat your dinner."

"Can I sit next to Daddy?" he asks, wide-eyed.

My eyes dart to Tane, who can't hide his amazed expression at Parker's question. I offer him a small smile, which after a few moments he returns. I have never heard him refer to Tane as that before. I never thought I'd see the day when Parker would call Tane his father, and this is a memory I won't be forgetting.

"Sure, of course you can," I tell him, giving him a gentle smile.

Tane smiles at me gratefully. *Thank you*, he mouths.

I nod and sit down at the table. *I better get used to this.*

"Mum, what time is Justin coming tomorrow?" Parker asks around a mouth of food.

My lips tighten. "He can't come tomorrow. I think he's a little busy."

Or his mum is a selfish bitch who wants your dad, and is now acting like a spoiled child who got her favourite toy taken away.

Tane tilts his head and watches me. "What happened?"

I look at Parker and try to answer. "Keira wasn't too happy after …"

Tane's jaw ticks. "You have got to be kidding me."

I shake my head no.

"I'm sorry Giselle," he says. "If I'd had any idea that you two were connected …"

He would have found someone else to sleep with?

I lift my shoulder in a shrug. "It's done. We usually spend every Saturday with Justin, so this is going to suck."

"I will handle it," Tane announces, a sharp edge to his tone. I'm sure he will.

"Don't worry about it. I'll call Levi, he will handle it for me," I tell him, placing my fork down on my plate. The air in the room suddenly turns dense.

"I will handle it," he repeats, looking down at his plate.

Okaaaaayy then.

I don't know why, but I push. "It's his sister, I'm sure he can handle the situation better than anyone else."

Tane's hands curl into fists on the table. "This is my family, and I will take care of it, no one else."

I raise an eyebrow, wanting to say something, but not wanting to start a fight with Parker present.

Tane doesn't look up at me to see my reaction. I sigh, pick up my fork and continue to eat.

"I want to play with Justin," Parker speaks up into the silence.

"Justin will come over to play. Don't worry, Parker," Tane says in a calm tone.

"Okay," Parker replies, grinning widely.

We eat the rest of the meal in silence.

"Thanks for dinner," Tane says when he's finished. "I'll clean up since you cooked."

"It's okay—" I try to protest, but he starts collecting the plates and taking them to the kitchen. He empties the plates, rinses them, and loads them into the dishwasher, then he wipes down the counter and puts the rest of the food away.

I can't help but find it strange to see Tane Miller cleaning my kitchen while I sit at the table with our son. I mean, seventeen-year-old me would have been fantasising about this very moment … I guess she just wouldn't have considered all the baggage and complications that the fantasy would come with.

"I'll give Parker a bath," I say, standing up.

"I'll give him a bath. Why don't you relax for a little while?"

"Tane—"

"I have a lot of making up to do. Can't you just let me feel useful for a little while? Please?"

"Well, when you put it like that …" I mumble.

His green eyes sparkle. "Come on, Parker, let's give you a bath and get you ready for bed."

Parker slides off the chair and follows behind his father.

"His towel and pyjamas are hanging on his door," I call out.

Looks like this co-parenting thing isn't going so bad after all.

*****

Tane

Time to handle this shit. The next day I pick up my phone, ready to sort this whole situation out.

I dial her number after I get it from Giselle. It rings three times before she answers.

"Hello," she says.

"Keira, it's me, Tane, from the other—"

"Oh, hey, Tane," she says, cutting me off. "I was wondering when you'd call." I'm guessing that saccharine tone was supposed to come across as seductive, but it makes me grind my teeth in annoyance. When I met her at a bar and she'd suggested we go back to her place, I'd thought *why the hell not?*

I'd take it back if I could.

"Yeah, sorry about that. Look, I had no idea you were Levi's sister and that you knew Giselle," I start off by saying. I try to continue but she cuts me off again.

"Well, I did tell you I was Levi's sister, but I guess you were preoccupied." Her voice goes low and I want to laugh at her suggestive tone. I wasn't preoccupied; I was bored.

"Anyway, I'm really sorry for leading you on or whatever, and I hope we can be friends," I say. I don't really mean it, but I figure I could try for Parker. I know he loves Justin.

"Friends?" she asks incredulously.

"Giselle told me you wouldn't let Justin hang out with them, and I was hoping you'd change your mind," I say, hating having to suck up to her.

"No, I don't think so. I don't want Giselle's negative energy to affect Justin." What the fuck does that even mean?

"Parker really misses Justin, and I bet Justin feels the same." The silence tells me that it's true. "And look, it keeps your Saturdays free to go out and do your own thing. I bet you could use the break." I doubt she puts one-tenth of the effort into raising her son as Giselle does, but I need to make this better.

"It is tiring," she admits. "Okay, fine. But if I hear of anything shady happening, the play dates end."

"Everything will be fine, Keira," I say soothingly. "Thank you."

"So, are we going to hook up again?" she asks. The suddenness with which she changes the subject surprises me.

"No," I say. "Just friends."

I want to tell her *no way in hell,* because I'm in love with Giselle, and I won't be touching anyone else. But then she will probably retract letting Justin come over.

"Friends can fuck," she says bluntly. I cringe.

"Not these friends," I say. "I gotta go, thanks. I'll tell Giselle to pick Justin up on Saturday." I hang up, not able to endure that woman's tenacity any longer.

Chapter Eleven

One month later

Giselle

I puff out a sigh as he keeps staring at me. "Excuse me."

He doesn't move. "Just one date."

I purse my lips and lift my face to look at him properly. Not bad looking, maybe thirty. This is the third time he's asked me out. He seems nice, but his persistence is a bit grating.

"I'm sorry," I reply, shaking my head, embarrassment heating my cheeks. A few people are looking at our exchange.

"Are you taken?" he asks, looking at my hand. For a ring, maybe? I want to laugh. My ring finger has seen less action than a nun.

"No, I'm not taken. But I'm not looking to date anyone right now," I lie, trying to get him off my back. I force a smile and try to walk past him when he gently holds my wrist. Not in an aggressive way, but still, he has no right touching me. I tug my wrist out of his hold, and put my hand up.

"I'm sorry, but the answer is no," I tell him in a stern tone. He needs to know I'm not playing any games, trying to act hard-to-get, or whatever. And no means no.

"Do we have a problem here?" an ice-cold voice comes from behind me.

Tane.

I spin to him and stare wide-eyed as he storms towards me in a few quick steps. "You okay?"

I nod, but take a step closer to him. An action Tane notices.

"I suggest you keep your hands to yourself," Tane tells the man, eyes narrowed on him.

The man shrugs, taking in Tane's size and demeanour. "Can't blame a man for trying."

"Well, try again and see what happens," Tane threatens, staring the man down. The guy nods and leaves the library.

Tane spins to me. "I don't like you being here alone."

I pull in a breath. "I'm not here alone, there's another librarian somewhere around the shelves."

"Giselle …"

"What?"

"I don't like it, is what," he growls, crossing his arms over his chest.

"It's a library, Tane," I say monotonously, "not a male prison."

"What did he want?"

"A date."

His eyebrows rise. "And you said …"

My eyes narrow slightly at his tone. "I said no, considering he was accosting me. What the hell do you think I said?"

Did it seem like I was interested? Was me pulling my hand away not enough of a reaction for him?

He sighs. "I'm sorry, I'm just angry. I didn't like seeing him touch you."

I rub my wrist. "Well learn to control it. What are you doing here anyway?"

"I thought I'd pick you up and take you out for dinner," he says, looking at me hopefully.

"Why are we having dinner?" I ask, nibbling on my lower lip.

"I thought we could talk. Parker is with Gage," he replies, pale-green eyes watching, dropping to my lips.

Alone-time with Tane is a bad idea.

I can't get involved with him that way, and it's hard being around him and having to fight my feelings. The way we have things now is perfect for all of those involved. Parker gets to see his dad and spend time with both of us, and I get to keep my heart intact. In some ways I trust Tane, and in other ways I don't trust him at all. I'm confused. All I know is that things have to stay as they are now.

Uncomplicated.

Safe.

"Look, Tane, I don't think that's a good idea," I say.

"Why not?" he asks.

"Ummmm," I mutter, trying to think of an excuse.

"It's just dinner, Giselle," Tane says softly, looking down.

Oh hell.

"Okay, dinner sounds good," I reply, mustering a smile. I never want to see him upset. Surely there's a middle ground?

"What time are you finished?" he asks, shifting his feet.

I glance at the clock on the wall. "In about thirty minutes. Do you want to sit here and wait?"

"Yeah," he replies, scanning the library. "I'll read something."

I grin. "Okay."

He loves reading, maybe even more than I do. He goes and browses the shelves while I finish up with my work.

"You can head home. I'll close up," Kate, my co-worker, says.

My gaze darts to Tane who is reading *DJing for Dummies*. I laugh when he flashes me a cheeky look.

I smile widely as I reply, "That would be great, thanks Kate."

I walk over to Tane and tilt my head to the side. "I'm pretty sure you already know that."

He laughs, a smooth sound, and closes the book. "I was curious about what it said. Plus, you're the one who suggested them for me."

"Smartass." I hold my hand out. "Want me to put it away?"

He stands. "It's okay, I can do it."

I put on my red cardigan as he returns the book.

"Where are we going?" I ask as we walk to my car. "I'll follow you."

He frowns like he doesn't like that idea but doesn't push me on it. "I thought we could try out that new place on William Street. The Italian one."

I love Italian food, and he knows it. "Sounds good."

I unlock my car door and get in. I watch Tane do the same, and then follow his car to the restaurant. We park right next to each other, and he gets out first to open my door.

"Thanks," I say as I get out, close the door, and stand right in front of him. I look up into his handsome face as he places his hand on my lower back.

"Come on," he says with an amused smile when I don't move.

Why is he so … Tane-ish? I like everything about him, and I don't even know why. Okay, maybe not *everything*, but still. It's like I'm hanging onto my young image of him, and whenever his behaviour matches that image I fall deeper into his trap.

My heart is being stubborn and won't let him go. Or let him in, either.

We get seated near the window, and then look over the menu. I can feel his eyes on me, but I keep my gaze down.

"I'll have the carbonara," I tell him. "What are you going to get?"

I look up to see his eyes on me and not the menu. I raise an eyebrow, but he just smiles. When the waitress arrives, he orders for the both of us.

His phone buzzes, so he puts it on silent and then looks up at me. "I want to talk about us."

I instantly turn wary. "What about us? Everything is fine the way it is."

"You're not even a little bit curious if there could be something more between us?" he asks, resting his fist against his cheek.

Curious? "I don't think being curious is a good enough reason to get my heart broken again, do you?" I ask, unable to hide the bite in my tone.

"So you haven't forgiven me," he muses, nodding his head thoughtfully.

"No, I have forgiven you. I just haven't forgotten, nor will I ever," I return, quieting when our drinks are brought to the table.

"I don't want you to forget, but I want another chance," he says softly, watching me with my son's eyes.

I sigh. "Look, it's really not even about that. The way things are? I want them to stay that way. We can't go taking chances like this when we have Parker. We need to put him first."

"And you think that taking a chance with us will be bad for him?" he asks, staring me in the eyes. "What if it works out, Giselle?"

"What if it doesn't?" I counter.

"I don't want to live out the rest of my life wondering *what if*," he says. "Potential failure isn't a good enough reason not to try. What message does that send to Parker?"

Manipulative bastard.

"What about one date night a week? After a month, if you decide you don't want to give me a chance, I'll back off."

Do I want him to back off? I don't think I know what I want.

"Four dates?"

"Four dates," he replies, bobbing his head.

"Okay, deal."

His satisfied smile makes me slightly nervous. Four dates with Tane Miller.

I can survive that with my heart intact … right?

Chapter Twelve

Tane

I ignore the call from my personal assistant, Julia, who has been ringing non-stop. I don't know what she could possibly want to contact me for. I know it could be important, but I've taken leave. I've already said that I won't be making any appearances or doing any club events until I'm ready to. I need this break. It's the first time I've taken time off in years, and I know I've earned it.

I've been mixing some beats at home, in the studio I've set up just for me. They remind me of why I got into this industry in the first place: my love for music.

I love how a song can bring back memories. I love it even more when you connect to a song so much, you feel like that artist wrote it about you. I've been mixing samples of songs that remind me of Giselle with the beats of other tracks, blending the old and making something completely new.

Kind of like us.

I call it *Spin My Love*.

I listen to music as I get dressed. Tonight is my first date night with Giselle, and I'm so fucking thrilled she agreed to give me a chance. As I drive to her house, I try to calm my nerves. I need to change her mind about me. I park my car in her driveway and walk to her door, which opens before I can even knock.

"You're on time," she says in greeting, stepping out and locking it behind her. Her red dress is long-sleeved but short, showing off her shapely legs.

"You look beautiful," I tell her, my eyes greedily roaming over every inch of her.

She turns and smiles shyly. "Thank you. I wasn't sure where we were going so I hope I'm not overdressed."

She is definitely overdressed. I'd love to help her out with that and peel off every bit of clothing she's wearing. She looks fucking edible.

"You look perfect," I tell her, putting my hand on the small of her back and leading her to my car. I open the door and stare at her creamy thighs as she slides in.

"Enjoying yourself there?" she calls out dryly just before I close the door. I grin unrepentantly as I walk to the driver's side and hop in.

"Can you blame me?" I ask her as I start the car.

She turns to me and flashes a smirk. "Will you tell me where we're going now?"

"Where's the fun in that?"

"I don't like surprises," she says.

"You say you don't like surprises, but you actually do," I reply, gazing at her profile. "You just can't stand the anticipation."

At least, that's how I remember her.

I take her silence as confirmation that I'm right. Nice to know that some things haven't changed.

"I can't believe I'm on a date with you," she finally says with a strange laugh, wringing her hands. I reach over and take one hand in mine, stopping her nervous gesture.

"I'm still me, Giselle," I whisper, giving her hand a gentle squeeze.

"You are and you aren't," she replies, staring down at our entwined hands. "Why did you turn to drugs? Was it because of your mum?"

My hand grips the steering wheel. I hadn't expected her to be so blunt. Tension builds, as I remain silent.

"I guess that's not really first-date material," she backtracks.

"We have a kid together, so I guess we have different rules." I sigh. "I'll tell you what, at the end of each date I'll answer one question, and you can make it as brutal as you wish."

Giselle knew I handled it badly when my mother passed away, but she doesn't know the truth of what happened with my dad.

No one does, except my cousin Keiran.

Keeping it bottled up inside wasn't the smartest thing I've ever done. I let it fester; let it grow into something I couldn't control. That, mixed with my mother's death and leaving behind everyone I cared about, meant I wasn't in the best place.

I turned to drugs because I was weak. Thinking back to those times makes me feel ashamed, but it is what it is. I fucked up, but I believe I've paid for everything.

With interest.

Now I want to claim my life back and move forward.

She clears her throat. "I didn't mean to be brutal …"

"It's okay, Giselle. I have nothing to hide from you. I guess I just don't want you thinking even worse of me than you already do."

She doesn't bother denying it.

"I don't know if four questions are going to answer everything I want to know," she says.

"I guess I'll just have to take you on more dates then," I reply with a winning grin. "Is Parker staying the night with Gage or should we pick him up on the way home?"

"He's staying the night," Giselle replies. "Gage and Levi wanted to take him swimming tomorrow."

I'm thankful Gage and Levi have been there for Giselle and Parker, I really am. I'm still not sure if Levi is interested in her as more than a friend. I want to ask, but I'm almost scared of the answer.

"I really miss him when he's not around," I admit, clearing my throat. "Thank you for letting him spend time at my house."

She's quiet for a few moments before she answers. "He should have his dad in his life. I'm not going to take that away from him because you hurt me; I'm not that selfish. In the end what happened was completely between you and me and had nothing to do with him. It would be unfair to hold it against you, and it would punish Parker in the long-run. Ever since you found out you were a father you've been amazing, and Parker loves spending time with you."

I didn't mean for our date to turn so serious so fast. "I never meant to hurt you."

She doesn't reply. I decide to change the subject. "You going to get any more tattoos?"

"Why, you don't like them?" she replies, a little defensively.

I raise my eyebrows. "I think they're sexy as hell actually."

Something about a good girl covered in tattoos … it's hot. Or maybe it's just because it's her. She could probably stop washing her hair and wear a potato sack and I'd still think she was irresistible.

"Hmmmm," she replies mysteriously, not looking my way.

"What does that mean?" I ask her.

"Nothing," she says, before turning to face me. "Except I guess you must have liked them since you picked me out of all the women who wanted you that night."

That night.

Both the worst and best night of my life.

Worst because I hurt Giselle, and the best because we created Parker.

I need a fucking do-over of that night. I'd be sober at that club, and I'd treat Giselle like she deserves. I'd talk with her, and recognise her after a little while, realising why I was drawn to her in the first place.

Because she's always been mine.

How do I explain to her that she's always been mine without coming across like an overbearing Neanderthal?

Easy; I don't. I keep my mouth shut and pray that she sees me and realizes how good we can be together.

As we drive closer to where I'm taking her tonight, I hear her gasp. "No way."

I smile. "What, you don't like this place?"

I grab my phone and send a quick message to the waiter I hired, telling him I will be there in a minute.

"You know I love this place," she whispers, taking in the riverfront we used to play in when we were younger. "I haven't been here in years."

I park the car and open the door for her. Taking her hand, I walk her down to the water, where a candle-lit dinner is set. I pull out her chair and gesture for her to sit.

"How did you get all this stuff here?" she asks, glancing around curiously.

"Magic," I joke, taking my own seat.

"It's beautiful, Tane," she says, smiling at me. "I have to say I am pleasantly surprised, but you didn't need to do all this."

"I wanted to," I reply, pouring the red wine for her.

She picks up the glass and puts it to her lips. "Delicious."

"The food is from your favourite restaurant," I tell her, as she lifts the silver tray. There are steaks with peppered mushroom sauce, baby potatoes, and grilled asparagus.

She gasps. "From Revene? How the hell did you manage this?"

I grin at her, loving the reactions playing out on her face. "I have my ways."

"I'll bet you do," she says, shaking her head at my evasion before frowning. "Can we eat now? I'm starving."

She's fucking adorable.

"Yes, of course," I say, swallowing my laughter.

She takes a bite and moans, causing me to shift in my seat. As she wraps her mouth around her fork, I groan and look away.

What I wouldn't give to be that fork right now …

When she finishes her mouthful she looks up at me. "So tell me how you got into DJing. I mean, I know you've always been into music, but how did you go from playing at school dances to sold-out music festivals?"

"Well when I left Perth I went to stay with my cousin in London," I say. My body tenses as I think about Keiran, but I don't want to talk about that with her. Not now. Not when we're enjoying ourselves. "He knew a lot of people and got me a weekend gig at a pretty good club in Soho. After a few months, a scout offered me a place in a local music festival's line-up and I accepted. It went really well, and then the scouts kept coming."

It was weird, really. I'd been young as hell and all that attention and recognition had been a big shock. I definitely didn't deal with it as well as I could have.

"That must have been a massive change for you," Giselle says.

I nod. "Yeah it was pretty crazy. It was cool though, for a while. Things just got too hectic," I say. I decide to change the subject so she won't press further. "What about you? You always did say you wanted to be surrounded by books."

She laughs, pushing a stray strand of hair behind her ear. I seriously can't get used to how stunning she is. She doesn't even realise it. "I can't explain it; I just love it. I don't think anyone gets it, but it just makes me happy."

Her smile makes me smile. "That's all that matters." We finish our meal in comfortable silence.

Chapter Thirteen

Giselle

The evening seems to end too quickly. It feels good to be able to ask him questions I've wondered about over the last few years. On our way home, I remind him about what he promised.

"You said I get to ask you a question," I say, wringing my hands.

He groans. "I should have known you wouldn't forget."

"Tane—"

"Ask away," he says, cutting me off from telling him he didn't have to answer if he didn't want to.

My mind races. I have so many more questions I want to ask him, so many things I want to know. "After your mum passed away, you just left town. You hadn't even told anyone you were leaving until the day you showed up to say bye. I want to know why."

He exhales heavily, staying quiet for a few tense seconds. "After Mum died, I was hurting. You know how much I loved her; she was everything to me. I was a mama's boy, no point even trying to deny that."

I smile, because it was the truth. He loved his mum, and they had a great relationship, unlike what he had with his father. Their relationship was definitely strained.

"Anyway, after she passed away, Darren gets piss-drunk and gets into one of his moods. I flip out on him as well because I was just tired of his shit. Then he tells me that I'm not even his son. He was yelling about how he had to spend his life raising a kid that wasn't even his."

"No!" I gasp, his comment taking me off-guard. Darren wasn't his father? "How is that possible?"

"I don't even know, really," Tane admits. "He just said that he met my mum when she was already pregnant, fell in love with her and took me on for her. Well, Darren hadn't been quite that articulate, and I remember him saying he wished I'd died instead of her."

"Wait, what? Did he say who your father was?"

"Yeah he gave me a man's name, someone I've never heard of. Then he told me to get out, because now that Mum was gone he didn't have to put up with me anymore."

I make a choked sound. That bastard! How could someone be so cruel? Darren had been there for Tane's whole life. How could he just disregard him like that? The fact that he wasn't his biological son shouldn't have mattered. My heart breaks for Tane, but anger overrides my system.

"I better not see that bastard around town," I mutter.

Surprising me, Tane laughs.

"You know you were always welcome to come stay with us," I say, hating that he felt he had to leave town. Why wouldn't he come to us? He and Gage had been friends since primary school. My parents would have welcomed him without hesitation if he'd said he needed somewhere to stay.

He nods. "I know, I just … I just wanted to get away, you know? I was hurting. I wasn't thinking. I just wanted to escape."

I stay silent, thinking everything over. "Thank you for telling me," I finally say.

"I've never told anyone. No one else knows except my cousin, and now you."

My eyes widen at that. I feel like he's trusted me with a sacred piece of his past. "Your cousin?"

"Yeah, Keiran, I think you met him once when we were younger," he replies, clearing his throat.

I rack my brain. "I think I remember him. Blond hair and blue eyes?"

"Yeah," he replies, his voice sounding hoarse. I have a feeling this doesn't have a happy ending.

"Where does he live?" I ask.

"He lived in London." Past tense.

I should have known something was up by the way he was acting, but I kept asking questions. "Where does he live now?"

"He passed away last year," he says in a low tone, his voice laced with sadness and pain.

"I'm sorry," I whisper, brows furrowed. I wait quietly.

"Go ahead and ask," Tane says suddenly.

I turn to look at his profile. "What?"

"I know you want to ask how he died, so go ahead."

"Tane, you don't have to—"

"He died from a drug overdose," he continues, as if I hadn't said anything.

I look at his profile. His hands grip the steering wheel. "Tane, I'm so sorry."

"I was with him the night it happened."

My breath leaves me.

Shit.

I reach over and grip his thigh with my hand, a silent show of support.

"Don't comfort me, Giselle. I don't deserve it," he says quietly.

"Shut up Tane," I growl, squeezing his thigh.

He sighs and touches my hand with his own. "I didn't mean to ruin our date."

"You didn't, and I asked."

Was Tane taking drugs with his cousin that night? Is that why he feels like he doesn't deserve comfort? I want to ask, but I feel like this isn't the right time. Not when it's clear he's hurting.

I sigh, my heart feeling heavy. I still don't regret asking. I need to know these things about Tane, to understand him and get to know why he was how he was.

I'm not going to judge him.

At the end of the day he's still Tane, and everyone deserves a chance at redemption.

"I think this conversation shouldn't be included in what constitutes date number one," he suggests.

My lip twitches. "Deal."

*****

"Justin and Parker want to go to the beach," Levi says as he walks into his kitchen. I put down my glass of milk and grin at him.

"They do, or you do?"

His lip twitches. "All of us do. Are you coming?"

"Sure, give me ten minutes to get changed," I tell him, walking to the guest room and changing into my red bikini. I put a pair of black board-shorts over the bottom, then slide my feet into my polka-dot-printed thongs. I grab my beach bag, sunscreen and a couple of towels, along with Justin's and Parker's swimwear.

The kids have several changes of clothes that stay here. They spend so much time at Levi and Gage's that it's just more practical that way. Beach gear in particular is vital, since we always end up in swimwear, especially if Levi is involved.

I walk out and don't miss Levi's gaze lingering on my body. For the first time it makes me a little uncomfortable. I try not to dwell on it. I head into Gage's room where I find the two boys watching *Frozen*.

"Do you two want to go to the beach?" I ask them.

I take their screaming as a yes. After both of them are dressed, we get in Levi's car.

"So, how's things with Tane?" he asks casually, keeping his gaze straight ahead.

I shrug, even though he can't see the motion. "He's really good with Parker."

"That's not what I asked, Giselle," Levi says, followed by a sigh.

"We're not a couple, if that's what you're asking. He did take me out on a date the other night though," I add, because I don't want to lead him on. I don't want to hurt Levi. He is one of the most amazing men I've ever met; he just isn't for me. Whoever does land him will be one of the luckiest women in the world.

"So you're … dating, then?" he replies, disappointment lacing his voice.

"Levi …" I whisper.

"I know, I know," he replies. "It just sucks."

"Uncle Levi said a bad word," Parker calls out.

I roll my eyes. "Uncle Levi can say it. You can't."

"Well, that's not fair," he says from the back seat, sniffing.

"Nothing in life is fair," Levi says under his breath.

I sigh.

"I can see the water," Parker calls out, pointing towards the strip of blue visible ahead. Justin cheers with him.

Levi grins, and the atmosphere in the car turns playful. "Hope you two are ready to catch some waves."

More cheering.

I glance at Levi and smile at him. He smiles back, letting me know that no matter what we are going to be okay.

Chapter Fourteen

Giselle

Second-date night rolls around. This time I pick him up. He hadn't been happy about that, but I insisted. When I pull into his driveway, I have to admit his house is beautiful. Located right along the beach, it's simple yet modern. Elegant, almost. I get out of the car and approach the door. It opens before I can knock.

Tane looks fantastic. He's wearing dark jeans that are tucked into black boots. He's wearing a tight black V-neck that is partially covered by a denim long-sleeved button up. He leans down and kisses me on the cheek.

"You look great," I say with a smile.

"You look better," he responds with a wink. "Want a quick tour of my house?"

"Sure." I step in and am surprised by how homey the place is. "Did it come furnished?"

Tane smiles at me. "Why? You don't think I can choose tasteful furniture?"

"Well," I begin, "I'm sure you could if you really tried, I'm just doubtful."

He narrows his eyes at me playfully. "I picked it all out myself. I used catalogues, but it still counts."

"Ahhh," I say, nodding. "You copied it all from magazines, got it."

He pinches my butt lightly, and it's my turn to narrow my eyes at him. "Come on," he says, taking me through to the living area. It's gorgeous, with comfy suede couches and a big screen fitted on the wall. The kitchen is simple and spacious with little to no clutter. I'm not sure if he's a clean freak or just doesn't have much cooking equipment, but it makes me feel a little self-conscious about my small, compact kitchen.

When he takes me into the hall and we come to a door that reads *Parker* in cute blue letters, my heart skips a beat. He already decorated a room for Parker?

My breath leaves me when we enter. The room is beautiful. The indigo-coloured walls look amazing against all the matching white furniture. There is a carpet on the floor with a racetrack on it, and the cars and trains scattered around the place are evidence that Parker enjoys playing there. There is even a proper mini train-track.

I turn around and hug Tane. I can't help it. "It's amazing, Tane!"

His cheeks redden. "I'm glad you like it."

I look at the time. "We should get going."

"Alright," Tane says leading me out of the room. "So, what movie are we seeing?"

"It's a surprise," I say.

*****

"Next time I'm picking the movie," he announces as we drive home.

"I guess that's fair," I reply with a chuckle. Okay, so I didn't have to choose a chick flick, but I did it anyway. On purpose. "So I guess this means date night is over, and now I get to ask my question."

He chuckles. "Alright then. I've been bracing myself for this all night."

I take a deep breath before I talk. "When we had our one-night stand," I watch as he cringes, "to me it didn't feel like a night of meaningless sex. I don't know if it was just because it was you, but to me it felt more than that. What was going through your head that night?"

He swallows. "You probably won't believe me when I say this, and I did try to tell you this before, but you weren't like the others. I knew it. Something was different." He looks at me in earnest. "In the morning, I saw you lying there, hair all over the pillow. I thought it might be you. I hoped it was. The previous night was completely blurred and hazy, but I remembered flashes of it. Of your eyes. I went to get you breakfast. I didn't leave a note. I should have left a fucking note," he mutters the last few words to himself.

"Wait, you were going to come back to me in the morning?" I ask, my jaw dropping open. *You have got to be kidding me.*

He sighs. "I woke up and thought I was fucking dreaming. You looked so different. I thought maybe it was you, but I wasn't sure. Why would you have come to me without a word? I went and got us breakfast, but when I came back you were gone. Then I told myself it definitely wasn't you, because you would never just leave like that."

"Holy shit," I whisper.

"It was karma," he says, laughing without humour. "How many times had I done that to other women, and then the one woman I wanted to stay with …?"

"Hey, I didn't leave you. I thought you had walked out when you didn't return," I say defensively. "And there were no personal belongings in the room, what was I supposed to think?"

"I went around the corner to get food; I was probably only gone twenty minutes. There was a line. And I'd left my bag inside the mirrored sliding door."

We're both quiet after that, lost in our own thoughts.

"I'm glad you told me that," I finally say. It's nice to know that he felt something, *anything* that night. Still, it's a bit weird to wrap my head around, because technically, he didn't realise it was me. Still, I put that to the side and just embrace the fact that he had felt a connection.

"You know what, I have a question for you now," he says suddenly, making me feel a little nervous.

"Okay," I say unsurely.

"You and Levi: what's the deal with that?" he asks, and I cringe. I don't know why I'm surprised he's asking me about this, but I am.

I clear my throat. "When Parker was about one we dated for a while, but we decided we're better off as friends." *By we, I mean me.*

"How long did you date?" he asks in a tone that tells me he's none too pleased about my news.

"Six months?" I reply, making it sound like a question.

"So you slept together," he says to himself. "Great. I think it was better when I didn't know."

I completely agree with that statement. "It's in the past," I say softly. "We're trying to move forward, right?"

He nods, looking tense, but saying nothing. I puff out a breath and look out the window.

When we pull up at Gage's house to pick up Parker, Tane says, "How about on the next date night we take Parker with us?"

I smile. "I think that sounds great."

"Good because I have an idea."

"Are you going to share it with me?" I ask.

He grins. "Not yet, but Parker will love it."

Levi walks out holding Parker, and the smile drops from Tane's face. He opens the door to get out.

"I'll get Parker," I tell him quickly.

I get out of the car and open the back door to put Parker in his car seat. "Hey, Levi."

"Hey Giselle, you look beautiful, as always," he says, leaning into the car and buckling a sleeping Parker in his car seat. "Hey Tane."

"Levi," Tane replies shortly.

Oh, boy.

Levi flashes me a knowing grin. "How was date night?"

"Good, how was Parker?"

"A delight," Levi replies, shutting the door closed gently.

"Where's Gage?" I ask, looking behind him.

Levi coughs. "He had a date."

I gape. "No way. Like, an actual date?"

He laughs. "Yeah, flowers and all."

"Holy shit. I'm sorry; if I had known Gage had plans tonight I wouldn't have just left you to watch Parker."

"You know I don't mind," he says with a shrug. "I had no plans."

I offer him a small smile. "I better get going. I'll see you next weekend."

We say bye, and I get back into the car.

"He still wants you," Tane says when we're almost at his house.

"We're just friends," I reply. He's my family. How do I explain that? I won't ever turn my back on Levi. He and Gage were there for me when no one else was. Such loyalty and friendship should never be taken for granted.

"Will you stay the night?" he asks as we pull into his driveway.

When I hesitate, he adds, "Just to sleep."

"Okay," I reply. We're already at his house. It makes sense, right?

Tane carries Parker as I take his keys and unlock the front door, then tuck him in bed.

"Do you have a t-shirt I can sleep in?" I ask him a little shyly. He smiles and pulls me by my hand into his bedroom. I look around as he digs into his drawer, finally pulling out a worn blue t-shirt that I recognise instantly.

"I can't believe you still have that," I say, pulling it from his hands. It used to be my favourite t-shirt of his, back when he was seventeen. I lift it to my nose and smell it. "I love this shirt."

"I remember," he says, chuckling.

I'm caught off-guard when he leans down and kisses my lips.

Wow.

My eyes flutter closed, but the kiss is finished before it began. The touch was brief, chaste, and sweet.

Tender.

It leaves me wanting more, but also feeling slightly dazed.

"You k … kissed me."

"I did, and I hope I can do it again soon," he says, eyes dancing with amusement. At my reaction, maybe?

I could get used to kissing Tane every day.

"Get changed. I'll make us some hot chocolate," he says, smiling at me before walking away.

I bring my fingers to my lips.

Then I smile.

*****

I lay in bed next to him, his arms wrapped around me and smile.

It's the best sleep I think I've ever had.

*****

I'm happy I don't have to wait until next week for the next date. Two dates in two days is breaking the agreement, but I don't even care. I can't hide the fact that I want to spend more time with Tane. Things are moving slowly, which is what I need, and I find myself thinking about him more and more.

Today he takes Parker and me to the water theme-park. It's hectic, people are everywhere, but I've never seen Parker have so much fun. He insists that Tane and I each hold one of his hands because that's what families do. It makes me so happy to see him so excited about having Tane in his life.

We take Parker on every ride. He even goes down the steepest water slides, though he refuses to go without Tane. Seeing Tane climb awkwardly onto the slides is hilarious; they definitely aren't designed for such a big body. After having lunch on the grass area, we go for a swim. Now we're chilling out eating ice creams.

"This was the funnest day ever," Parker calls out, face bright and excited.

"Funnest isn't a word," I try to explain, as he jumps up and down.

Tane laughs. "Told you he would love it. But I don't think this counts as a date."

"Why? Are you trying to get out of your question?" I ask, grinning at him. He's standing in front of me wearing nothing but a pair of black board-shorts, sitting low on his narrow hips. His body is lean and toned, like an athlete. He's caught me staring at him a few times but hasn't called me out on it … yet. My eyes once again roam over his smooth, tanned chest and his broad shoulders.

Fuck.

I clear my throat and look away and down at my ice cream. Much safer option.

"Are you ready to go home, buddy?" Tane asks his son.

"Dad! One more ride? Please?" Parker begs, using his puppy-dog eyes to his best ability.

"Okay," Tane says, smiling, before he looks to me. "Do you want to come or shall I quickly take him?"

"You can take him," I tell him, pointing at my melting ice cream.

His smile is warm. "We'll be right back."

I watch their retreating backs as they walk side by side, and I know I've made the right choice in letting Tane back into our lives.

Chapter Fifteen

Tane

We get home around seven o'clock, and Parker is beat.

"I'm just gonna put him to sleep. Make yourself comfortable," Giselle tells me with a smile.

"Do you mind if I do it?" I ask tentatively. I want to get used to doing these things.

She looks a bit surprised, but nods.

"Come on, little man," I say to Parker, who's standing there, rubbing his eyes. He comes and takes my hand and I lead him to his bedroom.

I change him into his pyjamas, not worrying about a bath since he had a rinse-off after the swim. I tuck him into bed and sit down on the small cushion next to it. I'm sure Giselle could sit comfortably on it, but for a man of my size it's a bit of a challenge to stay on.

"Daddy, are you going to come live here?" Parker asks, surprising me out of my balancing act. I fall off the cushion and look over at him.

I have no idea what to say.

"Why do you ask, Parker?" I bide my time, thinking of a way to answer. I don't want to give him false hope, but I don't want to crush that dream either.

"Bobby Pritchett's dad lives with him. I'd like you to live here. Then we could do fun stuff all the time, and you and mama could tuck me in," he says, the words rushing out of him.

"Well Bobby Pritchett is very lucky," I begin. "For now, I will still be living at my house on the beach, okay? Maybe it will change later, but for now let's just have lots of fun when we can, alright?"

Parker scrunches his nose in thought before nodding sleepily. "That's okay I guess."

"Shall we read a story?" I ask, hoping to cheer him up.

"Mm-kay," he says. I get about three pages in before he's fast asleep. I close the book and place it back on his bookshelf. Tiptoeing out of his room, I walk back into the kitchen where a freshly-showered Giselle is drinking a cup of coffee.

"I made you a cup," she says as the blows into her own.

"Thanks," I reply, sitting down on the stool next to her. "He's going to get a good night's sleep. He was exhausted." I don't mention the conversation with Parker to her. I don't want her to feel pressured, and I feel like I handled his questions well enough.

"I'll bet. Thanks for taking us out today. We both had a blast."

"So did I. We should do it again soon," I reply, then clear my throat. "You forgot to ask your question."

She smiles shyly. "I didn't forget. I've been thinking about what to ask."

"And?"

"And, I think I'd like to know about your cousin, Keiran," she says quietly. The temperature seems to drop a few degrees as that settles in the air.

I look down into my mug then place it on the table. "When I left Perth, I went to London to stay with him. He was good. I mean, he was loyal and caring, but he also had a bit of a wild side."

"So what happened?" she asks, leaning her elbows on the table.

"I told you about how I started DJing at one of the local clubs there. Keiran was already dabbling in drugs when I moved in with him, but when we entered the club scene it got worse. I got better and better at mixing tracks and producing, working my way up, and started playing at some of the best clubs all over Europe."

I pause, inhaling and exhaling deeply. "Drugs, women, money ... At first it was just a few E pills. Then we were heavy on coke. We were barely sleeping for days at a time. The pills we were taking to come down just weren't cutting it anymore, and then at one festival we were offered heroin. That was always my hard limit, but I was so out of my mind that night, I tried it. We agreed, just this once. It numbed my pain unlike anything I'd ever had ... One time turned into ... more than once ..."

She puts her hand on my shoulder and gives it a little squeeze.

"He died of an overdose after one of my sets. He had left early with a woman, and when I walked back into our hotel room I found him dead. His pants were around his ankles and he was lying on the bathroom floor. It was ... sad, really. That's when I knew I had to get my shit together; that I couldn't live like that anymore. I went to rehab for six months, and when I got out I came back here to take a break from everything."

I swallow hard as I let her process this. I'm surprised when she puts her mug down and lays her head on my shoulder, wrapping her arms around my waist.

"You're doing so well," she praises me in a soft tone.

"I have two reasons not to screw up now," I say against her hair.

"Two?" she asks.

"You and Parker," I reply. "I don't want to disappoint either one of you, or let you down. I want to be a father that he can be proud of. I *will* be a father that he can be proud of."

"I know you will," she replies, pulling away and wiping her eyes.

"Don't cry," I whisper, hating to see her upset. "I'm also going to make sure I can be everything *you* deserve."

"You need to want it for yourself more than anything, Tane," she says softly. "I think that's the only way you're going to beat this thing long-term."

I think that over. "You're right."

She forces a trembling smile. "I just never thought this would happen to us, you know? To be apart for so long, and to have all these things happen to you … I just wish you were here with me that whole time instead, because I never would have given up on you."

You don't deserve her.

I push away the thought and wrap my arms around her tighter, her body pushed up against mine.

"We're gonna be okay," she says.

I nod, hoping that she's right. I know I don't deserve her, or Parker, not after everything that I did. What I do know is that I will spend the rest of my life making it up to the both of them.

And I intend to do just that.

*****

"I'm assuming Giselle told you about us then," Levi says before sipping his drink whilst eyeing me over the rim of the glass.

How did he know? Every time I looked at him I wanted to punch him in the face for touching my woman. I'm guessing he could tell. Was I that obvious?

"She did," I say in a careful tone. "I know it's not fair for me to hold that against you, and don't get me wrong, because I'm so fucking grateful you were there for her, but I'm also jealous."

I put the truth out there; no bullshit. Complete honesty.

Levi nods. "I get that. You weren't here; I was. I love Giselle, but she's always loved you. Even when you didn't deserve it, which was most of the time. Her and I are nothing but friends now, but I'm telling you, that will never change. We will always be in each other's lives. I consider you a friend too, so I'm hoping we can all be okay."

And I get pure honesty in return—I can respect that. "I know Giselle loves you, my son loves you ... and hell, you have been my friend since I can remember," I tell him, struggling to find the right words to say. "As long as you realize you and her are only friends, then I think we can be cool."

He pauses for a second, but then nods with a little grin on his face. I'm jealous, but I need to let it go, because I have no right to be. He was here, I wasn't. That's on me, no one else. The consequences are mine and mine alone. My burdens to bear.

"Be good to her," he says finally.

"Fuck, man, I never want to hurt her again," I admit.

The door opens and Gage walks in with a woman, holding her hand. "Hey guys," he says when he sees us. "This is Bianca."

The cute, petite blonde waves at us. "Nice to meet you." Her voice is soft and sweet. She definitely doesn't seem like Gage's usual type, but I guess that's changed.

We mumble our replies as they head into his room. My eyebrows hitting my hairline, I turn to Levi. "Serious?"

"As serious as he's ever been before," Levi replies with a smirk. "First time he's brought her home, though."

Good for him.

"Keira told me about how you called her," Levi says. "Thanks for handling that. I wouldn't have let her try and keep Justin away."

My lips tighten at just the thought of her. How had I even touched a woman that was so selfish? "I didn't want Parker to have to suffer because I decided to …"

Did Levi even know about Keira and me? I don't think he did, and I wanted to keep it that way.

He shakes his head. "My sister is a troublemaker; always has been, and always will be. She's always been jealous of Giselle."

I turn to him. "Do you want to get out of here?"

"Sounds like a good idea." Levi laughs as giggling sounds come from Gage's room. We stand up and leave as quickly as we can.

Chapter Sixteen

Tane

I call Giselle's phone the next day, but she doesn't answer. Assuming she must be busy, I decide to go to the cemetery with flowers for my mother's gravestone. I stare down at her name engraved in the marble. *Jocelyn Miller*. I wish she could have been alive to meet Parker. She would have adored him.

Besides her taste in men, my mother had no faults that I knew of. She was kind, loving, and sweet, and never had a mean thing to say about anyone. She would be the first person to offer anyone help, whether they deserved it or not. She didn't deserve to die so young.

A heart attack.

I place the orchids on top of the headstone and take a step back.

I love you, Mum.

"I heard you were back." A voice I'd hoped I'd never have to hear again.

I turn and stare at the man who I thought was my father my whole childhood.

"I still come by here every week," he says when I stay silent.

What does he want? A fucking medal?

"I have nothing to say to you," I say quietly, turning and walking away.

"Tane," he calls out.

I turn back and stare him down. A man I thought was big and scary as a child is now shorter than me, slightly overweight, and looking a little worse for wear.

He looks pathetic.

I don't feel anything for him other than pity and hate. I know I need to forgive him—not for him, but for myself. I know how hate eats at you, making you do things you normally wouldn't.

"Did you ever find your biological father?" he has the audacity to ask.

Jim Carlson. The name of my father.

Did I seek him out? Yes, I did. But I didn't talk to him.

He's the president of a local motorcycle club. I sat and watched him with his wife, and they looked happy. I didn't want to ruin that. I don't know if he has other kids or not, or if he even knows about me, but I let it be. Besides, the last thing I need is to get caught up in the life of an MC world. Giselle might take Parker and run. And I really don't need to be around any drugs.

"I'm sorry, you know, for what I said to you," he finally says.

I nod, but it's a little too late for apologies.

"I still consider myself your father," he says quietly.

Really? How can he say that after how he treated me?

"I don't have a father," I call out as I turn around and walk to my car.

*****

I have a talk on the phone with my sponsor, Timothy. We check in with each other weekly, or more, if I need someone to talk to. After seeing my father, or at least, the man I'd thought was my father, I called him. We talk for half an hour, and he says the things I need to hear. I don't need to go backwards just because I ran into him. I'm stronger than that. Just because he pushed me away doesn't mean I'm not worthy.

I hit the gym for two hours then head back home. When I see my personal assistant standing at my front door, I frown, thinking something must be wrong.

"Julia?" I call out as I walk to her. "What are you doing here?"

She lifts her face up and smiles as she sees me. "I was getting bored on leave. I thought we could talk about some of the events you've been asked to do."

I wish I could say I wasn't a cliché bastard and that I didn't sleep with my assistant, but I can't. It was, however, a one-time mistake that happened when I was drunk. That might not be an excuse, but it's an explanation. I told her after that it wouldn't be happening again. She's good at what she does, although she can be pushy if you give her an inch.

Pun not intended.

"You're on holiday, Julia, we can talk work in a few months' time," I say. She's holding a clipboard in front of her, and looking professional in white and black, her staple black-framed glasses perched on her nose. "I can't believe you flew all the way here."

"I live in Sydney, not the other side of the world," she replies, rolling her eyes.

I sigh. I don't think she's getting the point. I pause. "How did you even know where I lived?"

"Tane, I'm the one that booked the real-estate appointments for you."

Oh, right.

I pull out my keys slowly, really not wanting to open the door. I cannot see this ending well, and I don't need any more points against me.

"Look Julia, why don't you go stay at a hotel, enjoy yourself, and we can talk work soon," I tell her, trying to act casual about it.

"Tane, I've missed you," she says, pouting slightly.

And there it is.

"We've spoken about this before …"

"I know," she replies. "I know you said we aren't anything to each other, but at least I still got to see you all the time. Now I don't even get that."

"I'm your boss," I say. "It's unprofessional of you to just show up at my house unannounced when you know damn well I'm taking some time off."

"I was bored," she snaps, losing her composure for a second.

How is her boredom my problem? She's been paid to handle my PR and be my assistant; surely there is something she could do?

A thought occurs to me. "How did you get here?"

"I took a taxi from the airport."

Of course she did.

It's only then I see her mini-suitcase behind her. This is so fucking awkward.

"Let me make a phone call, then I'll drive you to a hotel," I tell her as I fumble with my keys. I unlock the front door and let her in.

"Help yourself to whatever you want," I tell her, gesturing to the fridge.

"Okay," she replies as I walk into my bedroom, locking the door behind me. I pull out my phone and call Giselle, wanting to tell her what was going on here. Last thing I need is her thinking that I'm doing something behind her back. She doesn't pick up and I wonder what she and Parker are up to right now. Hopefully they are having more fun than me.

I call again with no answer, so I open my door, ready to get rid of my assistant.

When I hear Giselle's voice, I cringe.

Fuck.

I wish I could have told her what was going on so she didn't have to walk in on another woman in my house.

"Who the fuck are you?" I hear Julia ask in a bitchy tone.

"I'm Tane's girlfriend. Who are you?" Giselle snaps back.

She's mine? At least she's admitting it now.

Julie clucks her tongue. "Oh, honey, you won't believe how many women think they are Tane's …"

Like her, maybe?

"Sorry to inform you," she continues, "but Tane isn't the settling down type."

My cue to enter.

Giselle looks up and narrows her pretty eyes on me. Parker is nowhere in sight, thank God.

"She's my assistant, and she's just leaving," I tell Giselle. I walk over to Giselle and give her a kiss on her forehead, ignoring her stiff posture and dirty looks.

I turn to Julia. "This is Giselle, and she's a hell of a lot more than my girlfriend. She's the mother of my child and the woman I plan on marrying one day. If she will have me."

I hear Giselle's gasp. I sneak a look at her, hoping I haven't creeped her out. She looks surprised, her mouth dropping open. Julia, on the other hand, laughs cattily. "Yeah, right."

"That's enough," I snap. "Julia I'll call you a taxi."

I pull out my phone and do just that, leaving her gaping at the fact I wasn't even going to drive her to a hotel now. What I really wanted to do was fire her ass so I never had to see her again.

I watch out of the corner of my eye as she stands up. "Do you know what? I quit. Try not to fuck your next assistant."

With that parting shot, she walks out the door, dragging her mini suitcase behind her. I turn to Giselle, who is staring at the spot Julia just departed.

"You were sleeping with your PA?" she asks, disappointment dripping from her tone.

"I slept with her once. Over a year ago," I explain. "Just after Keiran died."

It's not an excuse, but an explanation. I clearly wasn't in my right mind.

"I see," she murmurs, staring down at the tattoos on her arm.

"Where's Parker?" I ask, changing the subject.

"Back at Gage's. We went to the beach today, and now we're having a BBQ. I came to see if you wanted to come."

And instead she got caught up in this.

"She just dropped by. I had no idea," I try to explain. "I'm sorry you had to see that."

"I'm sorry too," she bites outs, looking anywhere but at me. "I think I should go."

"Giselle—"

"Its fine, Tane," she replies, looking down. "I hate the thought of you touching another woman, but I know that it happened. A lot. Seeing it takes it to a whole different level though."

"Seeing it?"

"Seeing someone that you've slept with," she replies with a shrug. "We aren't even together; I have no right to feel anything."

"Oh?" I say, a smug grin appearing on my face. "Pretty sure you just called yourself my girlfriend."

"I was pissed off, Tane," she says dismissively.

"That's bullshit, and you know it. We always knew we would end up together, always."

She doesn't bother trying to deny it, but she does come back with, "If you always knew it, maybe you shouldn't have fucked around so much."

Ouch. The truth hurts sometimes.

"It's not as simple as that, is it?" I reply quietly.

She sighs. "I guess not. It's just not a good feeling to know so many women have had you. I know that I have to let it go, though. At least, the rational side of me knows that."

"And the other side of you?"

She raises a brow. "Don't tempt me."

"I'm sorry it hurts you, but to me they don't mean anything. No one matters to me except you," I say, my lips tightening in a slight grimace. "Julia was a huge mistake. I knew it the second after it happened. I'm sorry."

She sighs and walks up to me, placing her hands against my chest.

"Maybe we can still get our happily-ever-after," she replies, looking up at me.

Hope swirls in my chest.

"Yes, we can," I say softly, smiling. I wrap her in my arms, my fingers drifting down her back.

"You still owe me two more dates," she mumbles into my chest.

I chuckle. "You just want the questions, don't you?"

"I like the dates too."

"You think the dates will ever stop? Because they won't. I won't ever stop showing you how thankful I am to have you in my life, no matter how long we're together," I tell her.

She sighs contently. "I'll hold you to that."

"Come on. Let's go to Gage's," I tell her.

She lifts her head. "Should we wait for the taxi to come and pick up your assistant first?"

I can't help it; I laugh. She can't help but be kind and thoughtful.

"You better start looking for a new one," she tells me in a sharp tone.

"I will."

"A male."

"Yes ma'am."

She smiles. I grin.

All is right in the world.

Chapter Seventeen

Giselle

On our fourth date, Tane surprises me the most.

He tells me to dress up, and I do. I wear a black bodycon dress with a completely bare back. It reaches my knees, balancing out the show of skin. My hair is loosely curled and my makeup is simple. I love seeing his eyes roam over my body, widening slightly as he takes me in.

"You look incredible," he says, kissing my cheek. He opens the passenger door for me and I climb in.

"So, where are we going?" I ask once he gets into the driver's seat.

"Be patient," he says, making me narrow my eyes at him.

When we pull in front of the Hilton, I'm confused. A lot of people are walking in, all dressed to the nines.

"It's a fundraiser for breast cancer," he explains as we walk into the hotel lobby. "And I am going to play." I can't help but feel proud of him.

"Did they ask you?"

"Yes, my new personal assistant," he looks at me with an amused expression as he says it, "told me they had contacted her. She said I was on a break but would ask me. It's for charity, and I'm doing nothing, so why not."

Great. Another female personal assistant. I put that aside, because I trust him.

I smile up at him. "I think it's great. How do they raise the money?"

"Entrance tickets and food—all the proceeds go to charity."

We walk into a function room and I watch Tane set up. He looks so sexy, brow furrowed in concentration as he sets up his fancy laptop and equipment. A lock of his dark hair falls on his forehead and he pushes it away agitatedly. I grin against my wine glass. He doesn't even realise how sexy he is. A few minutes later he walks over to me, flashing me an apologetic look.

"I'm sorry," he says. "I don't want you to spend the whole night alone."

"It's okay. I'm happy to be here, seeing you in your element."

His green eyes turn soft. "I'm glad you're here too, and I hope you like it. I don't think I've ever wanted to impress someone more in my life."

I laugh at that, my eyes crinkling. "I'm already impressed, so you don't have to worry about a thing."

"Have any requests for me?" he asks, raising an eyebrow.

"None that you would enjoy," I reply with a giggle. "What will you be playing tonight?"

"Tonight I'll be playing a mash up of mainly mainstream music that everyone will know and have fun dancing to."

"Probably a good idea," I reply, taking another sip. "Can I ask you something?"

"Sure," he says, leaning closer to me.

"I know that you don't drink, but does it bother you that I do? You've never said anything about it."

"I don't mind if you drink. My issues are my own; I don't expect you to change. Also, I'm always around people who drink. It kinda comes with the job. I can't expect every single person around me to stop," he replies, pulling on a lock of my hair.

"Okay, but if it did bother you, or tempt you in any way, it's not a big deal for me to stop," I tell him.

His smile hits his eyes. "I know and thank you for that, but it's not necessary."

The hall starts to fill with people, and dinner is soon served. We take our seats at our assigned tables, marked by tiny little placards inscribed with our names daintily placed. There are various forks, which always makes me nervous, but I push that aside.

Moments later, our food is served. The meals are extremely fancy and well presented. There were two set options, I chose one and Tane chose the other.

"How is it?" Tane asks as I take the first bite.

I close my eyes. "Delicious."

He laughs. "Good."

"How's yours? For some reason you always end up ordering something tastier than me."

Every damn time.

His lip quirks up. "We can swap if you want."

"No, I'm good," I tell him.

He takes a few bites and looks at me with amusement. "Mine is definitely better."

Dammit.

"How would you know? You never even tasted mine," I ask, narrowing my eyes on him.

"Because nothing could be better than this," he replies after he chews and swallows another mouthful.

When his fork lifts to my lips, I look around to see if anyone is watching us. This is a posh place, and I feel a little weird about sharing food in front of everyone. When I see everyone concentrating on his or her own meal, I open my mouth and have a taste of his chicken.

Oh, God.

"It's not that great," I lie, looking down at my own, now unappetizing plate. His laugh carries throughout the room.

"Shhh," I reply, trying to stop my own laughter.

He lifts his plate and trades it with my own. "There you go."

"No," I say, trying to stop him. "You don't need to do that."

"I know, but I want to," he says dismissively. "So shush, and eat."

"Thanks," I tell him with a small smile.

We finish eating and then Tane gets up to play his set. I sit on a stool next to him and watch as people start to dance and enjoy the music. A few women come up and try to get his attention.

Standard.

"Are you okay?" he leans down and says into my ear.

"Yes, I'm good," I assure him.

Throughout his whole set, Tane samples songs that remind me of fond memories from our childhood together. I couldn't believe it when he dropped Sheryl Crow's "All I Wanna Do Is Have Some Fun". I used to sing that song twenty-four-seven. Tane used to hate it but I like that he remembered that I had loved it.

When his set is over, another DJ takes over, so Tane walks me to the dance floor. He pulls me up against his chest, one hand sliding down to my hip. He dances seductively, heavy-lidded eyes staring down at me as we move in sync. When he leans down and kisses me, I squeeze my eyes shut and kiss him back with everything I have. The kiss ends far too quickly, but we're in public, at a charity function. Now is not the time to explore this.

When I open my eyes the expression on his face is one of pure lust. I raise my hand onto his chest and push him back a little, so we aren't touching. His lip twitches as he takes my hand and leads me to a table.

We listen to the music until it's time to go. We're both quiet as he packs up and we drive home.

"You still have one question left, you know," he says.

"I know," I reply. "I've had it planned for a while now."

"Let's hear it then," he replies, sounding relaxed.

"I was wondering how you still have so much money. A drug habit is expensive, isn't it?"

Tane looks at me out of the corner of his eyes. "It is expensive, and I'd have a hell of a lot more money right now if I hadn't wasted so much of it. Luckily, I have people who work for me that suggested a few extremely profitable investments. And on top of DJing, I also produce, so that brings in extra money."

"People who work for you?" I ask.

"Yeah, a financial advisor and an accountant and what-not."

"Did they advise you not to spend your money on drugs?" I ask dryly.

He chuckles. "I'm sure they wanted to quit more than once, but they did make some good suggestions that I luckily listened to before I was too deep in shit."

"The money doesn't matter to me, you know. I was just curious, since you have a gorgeous house and car etcetera."

"I know," he replies. "The thought never once crossed my mind, Giselle. You wouldn't even take the money I tried to give you for child support throughout the years."

I'm really not that kind of person. I've worked for everything I have and will continue to do so.

"You know," he says, "this is our fourth date."

I smile. "I know."

"And do you think this could work?" His voice cracks a little. "Or are you going to tell me to leave you the hell alone?"

I puff out a breath. "I think we have a long way to go, but I'm willing to try and see where it takes us."

He exhales deeply. "I couldn't ask for anything more."

"It's not going to be easy …"

"Nothing worth it ever is."

Isn't that the truth?

When we get to my house, Tane walks me to my door. After I open it, he goes to say good night.

"Do you want to stay over?" I ask. He looks surprised. "Not like that … just to sleep again."

He gives me a soft smile. "I'd love to."

He locks his car and enters the house behind me. I set the alarm system and walk to the kitchen, then pull a jug of water from the fridge and pour two glasses, sliding one towards him. I down mine in several gulps and put the glass in the sink, while he sips on his. The silence is comfortable. I could get used to this.

When he's done I take the glass from him and leave it next to mine.

"Come on," I say, leading him to my bedroom. I feel a little nervous, even though I have no reason to. I'm not ready to have sex with him; I know that and he knows it too. But the idea of waking up next to him again … it's exciting.

I give him a smile before I go into the bathroom. I have a quick shower, washing the night off me, before drying and wrapping myself in a towel.

I walk out of the bathroom and hand him a fresh towel.

"Go ahead," I say. I don't miss the way his eyes run over my body, lingering on the droplets of water running down into my cleavage. It sends shivers of arousal through my body.

I hear the shower turn on so I drop my towel and get dressed. I pull on some silky pyjama pants and a plain camisole and jump into bed. I hear the shower turn off, and while I'm putting my hair into a braid, Tane walks out. My mouth goes dry. In nothing but boxers, he looks good enough to eat.

"Sorry," he says sheepishly. "I only have the button up." Heck, I'm tempted to tell him to ditch the boxers altogether.

Instead I say, "Don't be silly. Hop in."

He walks over to the bed and gently slides beside me. As I tie off my braid, I feel as though electricity is pulsing beneath my skin. The chemistry between us is insane, and we aren't even touching.

Tane lays down on his back before putting his arm out in invitation. He doesn't have to ask me twice. I cuddle into his chest, reaching my arm around him. I breathe out a long sigh. This feels amazing.

This feels right.

He leans down and gently kisses my forehead. I angle my head upwards and gently kiss his lips. We both let out a sigh.

"Good night, Giselle," he says.

"Good night, Tane," I whisper.

Chapter Eighteen

Giselle

"Hello," I say, answering my phone as I flop down on my bed.

"Hi Giselle," my mum says.

"Hey Ma, how's things?" She and Dad are enjoying their retirement in Boston. We try and talk to each other every month.

"Fantastic," she says enthusiastically. "Your dad and I have joined a country club and met a heap of people. It's a lot of fun. How are you?"

"I'm good, same old." I know she's just being polite, but this small-talk seems unnecessary.

"How's Parker?" I can tell she's trying, but I can't help but notice the way her voice tightens whenever she mentions him. She loves Parker, she does. She just wishes I'd waited another ten years to have him.

"Really good," I say. "He's happy and healthy."

"Have you met anyone?" she asks. "Parker needs a father."

I sigh. Here we go again.

"Tane is back in town, so we've been seeing each other." I won't lie, but I don't want to explain the whole situation to her. She pestered me enough when I was pregnant trying to find out who the father was. She lets out an excited gasp and I cringe.

"I always knew you two would end up together. How is he? Does Parker like him?" she asks. I am definitely not telling her that Tane is Parker's father. That's for another conversation.

"He's great and yep, Parker loves him," I say.

"Oh, that's great, honey," she says approvingly. "I'm happy for you. I have to go because your father is calling me, but I'll call later and you can tell me everything, okay?"

"Sure Mum," I say, happy to end the call.

"Love you," she says.

"Love you too." I hang up the phone. I'm not that close with my mum and dad. It's not that they weren't great parents, but we kind of lost our close relationship when Parker was born. I think they are enjoying their time to themselves, and that's okay with me.

I get up and walk into the living area where Tane is reading a book, his bare feet sticking out over the edge of the couch. My gaze moves upwards, taking in his strong thighs and his...

I lick my lips.

Get a grip Giselle.

It's been a week since we decided to see how things go as a couple. We're taking things slow, and I think we both need that. We need to build the foundation of our relationship before we go diving in head-first, but that doesn't mean I'm not feeling extremely sexually frustrated right now. Sleeping in his arms last night was a mixture of heaven and hell. Waking up with him curled around me was pure bliss, though the hardness that had been pressing against my thigh had been hard to walk away from. Pun intended.

"How's your book?" I ask him.

He lowers the worn paperback and stares at me, lip quirking.

"What?" I ask.

"Nothing, and it's good," he replies.

"What was that look for then?" I ask in confusion.

He grins wolfishly. "Nothing."

I look at the cover of his book. "What are you reading?"

He grins. "Do you want me to read some of it aloud?"

"Why? Is it porn?"

"No." He laughs. "It's a dystopian. I was just thinking that you look beautiful."

"Hmmm." It's all I say to that.

"Do you need me to do anything?" he asks.

"Why?"

"Just asking if there's anything I can do to help, is all."

"You look like you're enjoying your book. I have it covered. You can make dinner tonight, though," I tell him.

"Deal," he replies, smiling. He lifts the book back up.

"I do know the joy of a good book, you know," I say.

"So then you won't mind if I get back into it then?" he ask, hope in his voice.

I pick up a pillow from the couch and throw it at his head.

I shake my head and go check on Parker. I tiptoe into his room and see he's still fast asleep, with his mouth open and body sprawled across his entire bed.

Looks like it's a lazy Sunday for everyone.

I get a text message from Levi, which says him and Gage are going on a double-date tonight. I grin and put my phone on charge. I hope he finds someone who makes him happy.

Parker wakes up, and we take him to the park. Tane and he play football together while I take photos of the two of them.

Too much time has been missed, so I want to capture these moments as much as I can.

*****

I enter the house, tired as hell from my day of work, only to notice that the place is spotless. The scent of dinner cooking wafts towards me, and I take a deep breath. It smells delicious. I walk into the kitchen and see Tane and Parker playing with a new Lego set on the kitchen countertop as something simmers on the stove.

"I could get used to this," I call out as I enter, getting both of their attentions.

"Mum!" Parker yells, putting his arms out for a hug. I give him a warm cuddle and kiss him on the nose, then turn to Tane and give him a quick peck on the lips.

"What are you cooking?" I ask, peeping around him to see what's on the stove.

"Pasta, nothing fancy," he replies, lifting his hand up to gently cup my face. "How was work?"

"It was good. Same old," I tell him, lip twitching as I take in the domesticated scene in front of me. It's cute to think Tane is pretty much a stay-at-home dad—until he goes back to work, that is. I nibble on my bottom lip as I wonder what will happen when he does have to go back. More traveling for him, and Parker and I will have to manage without him again. The thought sucks, but I guess that's life.

"Sit down, babe, relax a little," Tane says, pulling me out of my thoughts.

"Let me have a quick shower first," I reply, rushing to the bathroom. I take a two-minute shower, not bothering to wash my hair, and then get dressed in my leopard-print pyjama set. When I return to the kitchen, the table is set and my plate served. I sit down and smile at the two of them.

"Thank you," I say, laughing at a grinning Parker who has pasta sauce all over this face.

"He was too hungry to wait for you," Tane says, sounding a little apologetic.

"That's okay," I reply. "You didn't have to wait either, you know." This wasn't some fancy dinner.

"I wanted to," he says, only now picking up his own fork.

"What did the two of you get up to today?" I ask after I swallow my first bite.

"Picked him up from kindy and then we went bowling," Tane replies.

I look to Parker. "Did you have fun?"

He nods his head enthusiastically. "Yes! I beat Daddy."

I look up into Tane's amused green eyes. "How did that happen?"

Tane grins wolfishly. "The better man won."

I squeeze Tane's thigh under the table, knowing he let Parker win—which I can't help but find endearing.

Tane flashes me a heated look, so I retract my hand because now isn't the time or place.

"Mum will you come with us next time? I want to beat you too," Parker says, shovelling another mouth of food.

Tane laughs at his comment while I bite the inside of my cheek. "Sure, I'll come next time."

Tane cleans up as I put Parker to bed, grateful to be able to spend this little bit of time with him. I read him a book, and he's asleep before I'm able to finish.

Tane is sitting on the couch when I leave Parker's room, humming a song, but stands up when I enter.

"What song were you humming?" I ask him. I swear it sounded like "Let it go" from *Frozen*.

"Nothing," he replies a little too quickly, a blush creeping on his cheeks.

I hide my smile. I guess Parker roped him into watching it. The kid is obsessed.

"Are you staying the night?" I ask him, fiddling with the hem of my top.

His Adam's apple bobs as he swallows. "Do you want me to?"

Do I want him to? I know if he stays tonight, we will be doing more than sleeping. The sexual energy is all but crackling between us.

I clear my throat. "I would like it. If you wanted to, of course—"

"Of course I want to," he cuts in. He closes the distance between us. "Just to be clear …"

"Yeah?" I ask breathlessly as his finger gently traces down my cheek.

"Are we just sleeping tonight?" he asks in a husky tone.

I want more tonight.

I'm ready.

As soon as I shake my head no, his lips come down on mine. His hand finds the nape of my neck, holding me in place as his tongue begs entrance to my mouth. He moans as I push my body against his, his other hand finding my hip. Walking me backwards until we hit my bedroom door, he lifts me up so my legs are wrapped around him.

"Are you sure?" he asks as he lays me back on my bed.

"Yes, I'm sure," I reply, distracted as I try to unbutton his pants. He catches my hand in his and waits until he has my full attention.

"I want you to be sure, Giselle. If you will regret this …"

I look into his eyes, letting him know how serious I am. "I won't regret this. I want this so bad."

"How bad?" he asks in a deep rumble.

"Why don't you have a look for yourself?" I reply sultrily.

He instantly slides down my silk shorts, a choked sound leaving his throat when he sees I'm not wearing any panties. He kisses my stomach, right above my belly button, then slides my top up. I raise my arms so he can get it over my head, leaving me completely bare before him. I try to see myself as he would be right now: breasts a little more than a handful, tattoos covering my arms and scripture on my ribs. Pale skin, a small waist that flares into wider hips and strong thighs, thanks to kickboxing.

"Beautiful," he breathes out, eyes roving over every inch of me. My face flushes at his perusal, but I hold my ground and don't attempt to cover myself up, even though the lamp is on in the room, and he can clearly see everything.

"Your turn," I whisper.

He pauses for a second, as if he doesn't want to take his eyes off me, but then starts to lift his t-shirt off. I take in every rippled muscle. The valley between his pecs begs to be licked, and I plan to oblige. I could never get sick of this view. I like it—a lot.

"And the pants," I manage to get out, still staring at his six-pack of spectacular abs.

He undoes his button, and my eyes don't leave his hands. The sound of the zipper lowering fills the room, then his jeans are pulled down his powerful thighs. He kicks them off, and allows me to stare at him, his lips twitching.

He's amazing.

He climbs onto the bed on his knees, bracing himself over me. When he lowers himself and kisses me, I close my eyes and just feel.

The kisses soon turn desperate, and his hands start to wander. His mouth lowers and finds my nipples, concentrating on one and then the other. I reach down and hold him with my hand, arching my hips up, silently begging for him to enter me.

"No rush," he admonishes gently as he starts to kiss down my stomach.

Okay, I do like where this is going.

At the first lick, I can't stop the moan that bursts from my mouth. How long has it been? Too fucking long. And now it's with Tane again. Nothing could be better than this—with him.

My hands thread through his hair and my head falls back against the pillow. To begin with, his licks are tantalisingly slow, but he slowly increases the speed.

"Tane," I whisper when I'm almost there. *So close.* He sucks on my clit and I explode, calling out his name as waves of pleasure take over me.

As I come back to myself, Tane leans over me once more, wiping his hand over his mouth and staring down at me.

I smile up at him, feeling relaxed and content.

"My turn," I suddenly say, rolling over him and licking my lips.

He makes a deep sound in his throat as I take him into my mouth. Relaxing my throat, I slide him in and out until he gently pushes my head away.

"I need to be inside you," he rasps, sitting up and pushing me back on the bed. "Condom?"

"I'm on the pill," I tell him.

"I'm clean," he says, as he slides home, making me moan. He's big and fills me, pleasure bordering the line of pain.

"Are you okay?" he asks, restraining himself.

"Yes, please," I beg, needing him to move inside me. He instantly complies, thrusting his hips in and out in sensual rhythm.

"You feel so good," he grits out, bracing his arms over me.

I pull his head down and kiss him with everything I have.

We finish together, panting and entangled. He kisses my forehead sweetly and then pulls out. I smile, my eyelids heavy, and snuggle into his body.

"Now that's how you make love." I sigh.

His chuckle makes my smile widen.

Chapter Nineteen

Tane

I wake her up with my mouth on her, then slide into her and make love to her slowly. Last night was incredible. I lost count how many times I reached for her in the night, wanting—no, needing to be inside of her.

She wasn't complaining.

"Morning," she mumbles sweetly after we both orgasm, a satisfied smile on her face as I gently pull out of her.

"Morning beautiful," I say as I stare down at her. Even just as she wakes, she is stunning. I don't think I've ever thought that of another woman before.

"I hope you're not that insatiable every night," she says, lip twitching.

I kiss her. "I don't remember you complaining."

She wraps her arms around my neck. "That's because I wasn't."

"I'll go make breakfast," I whisper against her swollen pink lips. "You can relax for a bit."

"Okay," she replies, kissing me first, then rolling over and burying her face in the pillow.

I smile as I exit the room, feeling a little ... proud? No, maybe satisfied that I could please her so much. I keep that thought to myself, not wanting Giselle to think I was some kind of caveman, but the feeling was there nonetheless.

I make some coffee then jump in the shower, humming as I do so. Once I'm dressed I wake Parker up and make him breakfast. I make some eggs, bacon, and toast for Giselle and bring it to her in bed. As she eats, I get Parker washed and dressed for kindy. I love doing all these little things for him. I guess in a way I'm trying to make up for lost time, but at the same time, I just like doing them. I like seeing him every day, and I like spending time with him.

Giselle walks out of the room fully dressed as I'm about to leave to drop Parker off. She's wearing all black, pants and a shirt, and these little boots I want to fuck her in.

"Thanks for getting him ready," she says, pushing her hair back behind her ears. She's got this red lipstick on that I want to kiss off her. She gives me a knowing smile. "Tane, we don't have time for that."

I bring her to me, lean down and kiss her neck. "Have a great day at work. Want to go out for dinner tonight?"

She sighs and nods. "Sounds good. You can choose a place. Parker likes Italian, though."

"Parker or you?" I ask, raising an eyebrow.

"Both of us," she replies, grinning. Then, she surprises me. She goes on her tiptoes and whispers in my ear, "How could it be possible to want you again? After how many times we made love last night and this morning?"

She pulls away, smiles, says *bye* to Parker and then walks out the door, leaving me open-mouthed and hard.

I shake my head and will my hard-on away.

That woman is going to be the death of me.

*****

I spend the morning talking to my new agent, Leanne, about getting a few gigs lined up for when I return to work, then head back to my house and spend a few hours in my studio room. It's been a few weeks since Giselle and I first slept together, and I've been at her house pretty much every night since. I want us to move in together, but I don't know if she's ready for it yet. I keep hoping she will bring it up—but no luck so far. I can be patient. When it comes to her, I know I can be patient. I open the top drawer in my study and pull out the small black, velvet jewellery box.

Soon.

I slide it back away and then stand, needing to get ready to pick Parker up from kindy. I told him I would take him surfing afterwards. I pick him up and then get some lunch on the way, dropping it off at the library for Giselle. After that we head to the beach, meeting Levi there. When I see Keira there with Justin I force a smile, but do my best to stay out of her way. Soon enough, though, she walks over in her tiny yellow bikini, sticking her chest out so obviously that I see Levi cringe. I'm pretty sure my expression mirrors his.

"How have you been, Tane?" she purrs, sliding next to me. I don't miss her staring at my body.

"Good," I reply, moving away from her and turning my attention to Parker.

Levi walks over and stares down at Keira. "Justin wants you to play with him."

Keira sighs, like it's an imposition, but goes over and plays with her son.

"Sorry," Levi says, grimacing. "I wanted to bring Justin but she found out you were coming and insisted she be here."

"It's alright," I tell him. "She is your sister."

Levi sighs heavily. "And you can't choose your family."

"No, but you can make your own."

He bobs his head, reflecting quietly. "I'm happy for you and Giselle."

I turn to him. "You are?"

"Of course I am. I've never seen her this happy before."

"I've never been this happy before." I smile. "Let's go catch some waves, shall we?"

He laughs. "Maybe some small waves, since we have the two boys. I don't think you want to leave Parker out here with Keira watching him."

Nope, definitely not.

"Small waves it is."

*****

Giselle

That night, Tane and I are in bed, my head on his chest. "Tane?"

"Yes?" he replies.

"Do you remember when you were sixteen and went on a date with Claire?" I ask.

He chuckles. "You still remember her name?"

I frown into the darkness. "Of course I do. She had her skinny arms all over you."

"You were fourteen …"

"So? I remember you and Gage bringing her and her friend to the house when Mum and Dad weren't home. I was so jealous—I was actually considering punching her in the face."

"Well, I'm glad you didn't," he says, sounding amused. "I was just a stupid horny kid back then."

"So you're admitting something happened that night?" I ask, my voice raising.

He clears his throat. "Are you going to get mad over something I did when I was sixteen?"

Yes. No. *Maybe.*

"That means yes," I mutter.

"Babe, you were young. And so was I," he says softly. "I wasn't thinking about how years from now, the woman I love would be busting my balls over it. All I was thinking about were boobs and ass."

I can't help it. I laugh.

"So she let you touch her boobs then huh?"

He makes a non-committal noise, which I take as "more than that."

"See, I should have punched her," I grate out.

"She kinda went down on me that night," he admits, holding me close so I can't move away. I elbow him in the stomach. "Ouch! I was just trying to be honest."

"Do you want to hear about my sexual history?" I ask.

He makes a growling sound. "Fuck no. I like to imagine I'm the only one you've ever been with."

I giggle at that. "See."

"It doesn't matter. The past is the past, and there is only one woman for me," he tells me. "You're stuck with me, Giselle, because I'm yours. And you sure as hell are mine."

I think I can live with that.

"You're here every night anyway. Why don't you just move in?" I blurt out.

He stills. "Are you sure that's what you want?"

I put my hand on his cheek. "Of course it is. Don't you?"

"I'd love to move in," he admits. "I wasn't sure if you felt the same way, and I didn't want to rush anything."

I kiss his lips. "Then it's settled. You're moving in with us."

"Okay," he whispers, kissing the top of my head.

"Oh, and Tane?" I say, lifting my head up.

"Yes?"

"I love you." More than anything.

"I love you too, Giselle," he replies softly.

Chapter Twenty

Giselle

"When are you going to move all your stuff over?" I ask Tane. It's been a week since we had the discussion, and I'm wondering if maybe he's dragging his feet for a reason. Did he not want to move in? Maybe I'm pushing too hard?

"I'll get everything on the weekend," he says.

I look around my much smaller house. "Are you okay with living here? I know it's nothing much compared to what you're used to."

"I'm happy here. If we need a bigger house we can buy one. Don't stress about it," he says, flashing me a boyish smile. "Ah, and there's something else. I don't think you're going to like it and you'll probably overreact …"

"What is it?" I ask, trying not to think the worst.

"Well, I kind of paid the mortgage off on this one."

I gasp. "You didn't?"

He grins. "Of course I did. I'm living here, aren't I? Did you think I wasn't going to contribute? I'm not a loser."

"You didn't?"

"I did," he replies. "You don't need to make a big deal out of it. You know I'm not hurting for money."

"That's beside the point, Tane!" I reply. I can't believe he did this. It's a nice, generous gesture, but a little over the top. Also, he should have spoken to me about it before he did it. Before he came back into our lives, I did everything myself and made all my own decisions for Parker and me. I'm not sure how I feel about this sudden loss of control.

"Giselle—"

"This is very generous but it's too much," I tell him, shaking my head. "How am I supposed to accept this?"

His eyes narrow on me. "This is why I wanted to surprise you. I knew you would be stubborn about it."

"So you knew I would have an issue with it but you still did it anyway?" I ask, placing a hand on my hip.

"I hoped that in time you would realise that I was trying to do something nice for you," he says after a long pause. "I'm not going to live here and not pay anything."

I roll my eyes. "No need to be dramatic. Contributing is one thing; paying off an entire mortgage is another!"

"Are you arguing just for the sake of it?" he asks, crossing his arms over his chest.

Am I? I have no mortgage anymore. I don't know whether to jump for joy or strangle him.

His eyes crinkle. "Is the fight over now? Can we make up?"

I laugh at his hopeful expression. "What did you have in mind?"

His eyes darken at my sultry tone. "You on the kitchen table? My face between your legs?"

My eyes widen at his dirty talk. "If you want me, Tane Miller, you're going to have to catch me."

I bolt through the hallway before I even finish the sentence. He catches me before I hit our bedroom, lifts me in the air and throws me over his shoulder like I weigh nothing. He slaps my ass, the sound echoing through the silence. Depositing me on our bed, he lifts up my skirt and pulls down my red panties without saying a word. Then, without further ado, his mouth is on me, licking and teasing until I come apart. His pants are off and then he's sliding into me before his lips capture mine, his tongue synchronising with his pelvic thrusts. I lift my hips up, silently begging for more. He rolls over, still inside me, leaving me straddling him. I get to work instantly, lifting and lowering my hips, taking from him just what I need. I lean my hands back on his hard thighs and let my head fall back, closing my eyes and losing myself in the moment. His thumb finds my sweet spot, and I come instantly, my hips jerking violently.

"Fuck, fuck, fuck." I mutter over and over. When the orgasm subsides, I fall onto his chest and smile.

"I'm not done with you yet," he growls, flipping me onto my back, and then onto my stomach. He lifts my hips up and slides back into my wetness. I moan into the mattress. Too much, but yet not enough. I thrust back against him a few times until he comes, moaning my name. He gently pulls out and rolls onto his back, taking me with him.

We're silent for a few moments, both getting our breath back.

"That was amazing," I tell him, placing a kiss on his chest.

He gives me a slow-spreading smile in return. "You're amazing."

"I love you," we say to each other at the same time.

Tane kisses me on the nose. "Thank you for giving me a chance to be this happy."

"Thank you for earning it," I reply. We stay in bed for about half an hour, just talking and playing around, then I slide out of bed and have a quick shower. Parker is with Gage for the night, so Tane and I have all night with each other.

I gasp when the shower-screen suddenly opens, and a very naked Tane walks in. "Mind if I join you?"

"Not at all," I whisper as he pushes me back against the shower wall.

Not at fucking all.

*****

Grabbing the belt loop of my jeans, Tane pulls me to him. "Where do you think you're going?"

"I have to get changed and then head to the gym for kickboxing," I explain a few days later.

"Am I not giving you enough workouts in the bedroom?" he jokes, his grin showing off his straight white teeth.

"No, you're not, maybe you need to work harder," I tell him in a sweet tone.

"I'll remember that tonight," he replies in a low rumble.

I lick my lips. "And I'll be looking forward to it."

"Can I come with you?" he asks in between kisses.

I smile against his mouth. "Sure. We have two hours until Parker needs to be picked up."

"Okay, let's get changed," he says, pulling away from me.

I miss him instantly.

We dress quickly, and I have to admit that Tane looks ridiculously good in his gym gear. The shorts are loose but the top is fitted, and my mouth goes dry looking at him. I strengthen my resolve and turn away, locking the house up before we both go outside and jump into Tane's car.

The gym is packed out, like it usually is. I head for the treadmill while Tane hits the weights. I'm just working up a sweat when Greg pops up in front of me.

"Hey, beautiful," he says in greeting. "Haven't seen you in a while."

"Been busy," I reply, forcing a small smile. I turn the treadmill setting to a low, walking speed. "How have you been?"

I only ask to be polite, which was a mistake, because he takes it as an invitation to talk about himself for as long as possible.

"What are you doing on Friday night? Do you want to go out for a drink?" he asks.

"Sorry, but I have a—"

"She's taken," Tane cuts in from behind us. I turn around and look into his heated gaze.

Shit. I turn off the treadmill.

Greg loses his smile. "I didn't know you had a boyfriend?"

I didn't know I had to tell him my whole life story.

"Well I do, I'm sorry," I tell him, trying to make this as least awkward as possible.

"What a shame," he murmurs, staring at my chest. "We could have had some fun."

"You have to be fucking kidding me," Tane growls, hands clenching into fists.

Uh-oh.

Greg turns to Tane. He's bulkier than Tane, but a lot shorter. He also should stop missing leg day, because his are kind of skinny, making him look disproportionate. I'd never noticed that before. "My bad."

"You better get the fuck out of here and away from my woman," Tane seethes.

"Tane …"

I'm ignored.

Greg smirks but leaves. Maybe he does have half a brain after all.

"How long has that fucker been after you?" Tane asks me.

I shrug. "He asked me out once and I said no. That's it."

That seems to calm him a little going by his now relaxed shoulders. "I'm going to the punching bags. Stay where I can see you."

Okaaayyy, then.

"Yes Sir," I reply sarcastically, turning the treadmill back on and getting back into my run. An hour passes, and then we have showers in the separate male and female areas.

When we walk out to the car, he speaks. "I'm sorry I snapped at you. I just didn't like him talking to you like that."

"I know," I reply.

He opens the car door for me. "The thought of another man near you … it makes me crazy."

I turn and grip his chin with my fingers. "I'm yours, and I want only you. You have no reason to be jealous."

His eyes search mine. "I don't know what I did to deserve you."

My lips curve. "You knocked me up." He shakes his head at me, and then kisses me senseless. "Was that supposed to teach me a lesson for my smart mouth?"

"No," he breathes. "I just couldn't wait another second without kissing you."

My mouth makes an *O* shape. That was sweet; really sweet.

"Let's go pick up our son," he says, stepping away from me.

I nod and get my ass into the car.

Chapter Twenty-one

Tane

The black box feels like a heavy weight in the pocket of my jeans. Feeling nervous and slightly flustered, I pace up and down, waiting for her to walk through the front door. My fingers tangle in my hair as I pull at the ends.

She wouldn't say no … would she?

The door opens and she walks in, smiling, happy to see me.

I hope that never changes.

"Hey," she says, closing the door with a cock of her hip. "Is everything okay?"

"Everything is fine," I say hoarsely, grabbing her small hand in mine and leading her through the house into our bedroom.

The room is filled with lit candles.

She gasps. "Tane it's beautiful."

I pull out the jewellery box, and open it so she can see the solitaire diamond ring. Another gasp. My fingers tremble, causing the box to shake slightly as she studies it in my palm. I get down on one knee.

Please say yes.

"Holy shit," she mutters, fanning her face with her hands; a very girly gesture. My lips twitch at her response.

"I love you, and I want to spend the rest of my life with you by my side. Will you marry me, Giselle?"

Her pouty mouth drops open, and her eyes shine with tears. "Yes, of course I will marry you."

I stand up and she jumps into my arms. I lift her off the ground. She kisses me roughly, her lips hard on mine, but I pull my face away. "Don't you want to put the ring on?"

The look on her face makes me feel a hundred metres tall. Like a king. Like a hero.

I'll do everything in my power for her to always look at me like that.

She smiles and allows me to lower her to the ground. "I love you."

"Well, you better," I tease, sliding the ring on her finger. I kiss the knuckle on her finger afterwards.

"It's beautiful," she says, staring at it in awe. She glances up at me. "I didn't need a rock the size of a small planet."

She doesn't need it, but she does deserve it.

Giselle is such a strong woman; she takes what life gives her and goes with it, never complaining, and always happy and grateful with what she has. I could never love anyone more.

"I'm glad you like it." Thrilled and relieved is more like it.

She glances around at the candles. "This is very romantic, Tane."

I clear my throat. "Can we have engagement sex now?"

"Well that lasted two minutes," she says playfully as she pulls her top off.

"I promise I'll last longer," I retort. My mouth dries at the sight of her, as it does every damn time.

And she's all mine.

Possessiveness rises in me. "Come here."

She steps to me, hips swaying. "Do you want something?"

Yes, I do. Her. Always her.

She's the only drug I will ever need for the rest of my life. The scary thing is she's far more addictive than anything I've ever done.

*****

"So you finally manned up," Gage says to me, looking amused. He knew I was proposing to Giselle, because I spoke to him about it first. I let him know that I wanted his approval but would ask her anyway without it. I know Gage is much closer to her than her father, which is why I asked him.

I slap him on his back. "You ready to be my bro-in-law?"

The corners of his eyes crinkle. "You've practically been my brother my whole life anyway. This is just making it so on paper."

I swallow. "You getting soft on me? I'm guessing this is Bianca's doing."

Gage sighs, running a hand through his hair. "There's something about her, you know?"

"So it's serious then?" I ask, touching the ocean water with the tip of my toes.

"Yeah, I think it is." He pauses. "I just hope her and Giselle get on."

"Well Giselle owes you for not kicking my ass more than you did," I joke, shielding the sun from my eyes with my hand.

"That's the truth. I'm glad it worked out for you both though. She and Parker deserve the best."

And I plan on giving that to them, for the rest of their lives.

"When's the wedding?" he asks as he sits down in the sand.

"She said next January. She needs time to plan, and she wants a beach wedding so she wants it during summer."

"She always did want a beach wedding," Gage muses.

"I remember," I add, thinking back to when Giselle was thirteen and raving on about her future wedding. "She said her bridesmaids were going to wear bikinis."

"I wonder if that still stands," he replies with a smirk.

"Why? Is Bianca going to be a bridesmaid?" I ask him.

"They don't even know each other yet!"

"Well, she doesn't have many other friends," I say. "Like she always tells me."

"True." Gage laughs. "Just Levi and me. And I'm her brother, so I don't even count."

"She said Ciara will fly down to be her maid-of-honour," I say.

"That's good," Gage replies, but I don't miss his slight grimace.

A chuckle escapes me. "You and Ciara?"

He groans and turns to look at me. "Once or twice. Or every day for a whole year."

I laugh at him, hard. "Will she start shit?"

Gage thinks it over. "I don't think so. I just don't want Bianca to be uncomfortable."

I make a whipping sound.

"Like you can talk," he grumbles. I ignore that. I'm way beyond whipped. They need to invent a whole new word to describe what I'm feeling.

"Will your parents come down for the wedding?" I ask. Giselle hasn't spoken much about them. I asked her a few times, but she just said that they try and keep in touch over the phone.

"I think they will," he says. "At least, they better."

"What happened?" I ask him.

"They just grew apart after Parker was born. They were angry, saying she was throwing her life away. Especially when she wouldn't tell them who the father was; they assumed she was sleeping around and didn't *know* who the father was. Words were said, and sometimes, no matter how sorry you are, you can't take words back. They leave an imprint."

My hands clench. "And I was off living my life while she was here dealing with all this shit."

"You didn't know, man."

I shake my head. "It doesn't matter. I'll never forgive myself."

"It's in the past. Let it go," he says sagely.

I hate that a certain song enters my head after he says those lines. On the plus side, it lightens my mood. Damn Disney.

"She's forgiven you; I think it's time you forgive yourself."

He's right. If only it were that easy.

We lay in the sun for a bit, then grab our surfboards and hit the water. Just like the old days.

Chapter Twenty-two

Tane

"Hello," I say, lifting my phone to my ear.

"Hi Tane, it's Leanne," says an assertive female voice.

"Hey Leanne, what's up?"

"Next week you're officially back to work, so I'm calling to go through a few prospective shows for you. There has been quite a few calls from people interested in having you play."

I sigh. I can't believe how much I'm dreading going back to work. I love what I do, but I love my family more. That realisation hits me pretty hard.

"Alright, give me the run down," I say, rubbing my brow.

*****

Giselle

"So, when will you be leaving?" I ask him. I can't hide my disappointment. I knew he'd have to go back to work eventually; heck, he'd told me enough times. Whenever it came up, I'd constantly put it to the side just because I didn't want to imagine what our lives would be like without him here. Parker and I had gotten used to having him in our little family—not that that will change. It's the day to day that will be different when he's traveling.

"Next Thursday," he says, his expression equally as forlorn. Nine days away.

I move closer to him, pressing my chest against his. "I'm going to miss you," I tell him as I wrap my arms around his neck.

"I'm going to miss you more," he says, bending down to press a kiss against my neck. "Both of you."

I let out a long regretful sigh. "This sucks."

"I'm so sorry, baby," he says. He looks forlorn, and it makes me feel bad. I don't want him to feel guilty for doing something he loves. I knew what I was getting into.

I muster up my best smile. "Don't be," I say, giving him a gentle kiss. "We'll make it work."

"You're amazing," he tells me. I run my hand through his hair, cupping him at the nape.

"No, you're amazing. You're the most amazing thing that's happened to Parker and me," I tell him earnestly. His eyes get glassy, and it makes my heart melt. This man is incredible.

I hope he knows how much.

*****

Tane

The loud music blares from the speakers as I bob my head to the beat. I look around the packed-out nightclub, watching people dancing. Drunken men laughing, and women who must be fucking cold, considering how little they are wearing, are scattered throughout the establishment. I used to love this environment, but now I'm not sure if I want to be here. I want to be with my family, with Giselle and Parker, not back in the same atmosphere that nearly killed me last time. My mind roams to the conversation we had yesterday, and the questions he asked me.

"Daddy, will you be going away again?" he asked.

"What do you mean? I have to go to work, but I will be back soon," I tried to explain.

He shrugs his tiny shoulders. "But I don't want to have no daddy again."

My heart broke with those few innocent little words.

I take a sip from my water and stare at the dance floor over the rim of my bottle. Nothing has changed.

I change the song, mixing it into The Aston Shuffle's "Comfortable". People cheer, letting me know it was a good choice. My lip kicks up at the corner at their reactions and their fist pumps. A few women hang out by the DJ booth. Nothing new there, except this time I don't pay them any attention. I smile politely but decline their offers to join them in their beds after my set is over.

I lay in my hotel bed that night, missing my family.

One week to go until I see them again.

*****

Giselle

"When's Daddy coming home?" Parker asks me, not for the first time.

"In a few days," I reply, serving him his dinner.

"How many days?" he asks, staring down at his plate.

"Three."

He sighs heavily, not happy.

"Time will go fast, don't worry," I tell him.

He doesn't reply.

"So, what did you do at kindy today?" I ask him, trying to get him talking.

"Painting," he replies. "I painted a picture of me and Daddy surfing."

Annnnddd here we go again.

We eat the rest of our dinner in silence as I watch my son sulk.

"Shall we get ready for bed?" I finally ask.

"Okay Mum," he says, sipping his water and then sliding off his chair.

I puff out a breath and follow him.

It's going to be a long few days.

*****

"He's in Sydney, not on the other side of the world," Levi says to me as I sit on his couch watching TV. Parker and Justin are fast asleep, tired from the day's events. A usual Saturday for me, minus Tane.

"I know that," I reply, taking a sip from my wine before putting the glass down on the coffee table. "I just miss him."

"You know," he starts, "I'm off for the next few days."

I turn to stare at his profile. "Okay?"

He looks at me, grinning boyishly. "You could go to Sydney and surprise Tane for his last two nights. Have a little fun. Gage and I will keep Parker."

My mind races. Is this a good idea? I don't want to get in Tane's way while he works, but the thought of seeing him …

"I don't know …"

"Parker will be fine. You know he loves it here with us," he says, watching me, waiting for me to say something.

"Of course he does. He's just been sulking since Tane left and …"

"He wasn't sulking today. He was too busy having fun."

That was the truth.

My phone beeps with a text.

Tane: Miss you so fucking much.

Miss you more, I reply.

"I guess I could go away for two nights," I say to myself.

Levi wraps an arm around me. "You should go. Have a little break."

I lean my head on his shoulder. "You're way too good to me."

"Well, with Gage always with his girlfriend, Parker and Justin have become my only friends," he jokes.

I make a scoffing sound. "What happened to your double date?"

He clears his throat uncomfortably. "It was fun, but it wasn't …"

"Permanent?"

"Oh, come on, Giselle, don't make me talk to you about these things," he begs.

"Why? It's been so long since we were together," I say. "I want you to talk to me about these things. Lord knows I dump all my issues on you."

He chews on his bottom lip. "You're right, it has, but it's still a little weird for me."

"You know I love you," I whisper. I'm just not in love with him.

"I know, and I love you too. And I'm happy for you and Tane."

"That's because you're amazing and unselfish."

He stills. "I'm not a saint."

I laugh. "Don't I know that. When will Gage be home?"

"I'm not sure, to be honest. I know he wants you to spend some time with Bianca."

"Yeah, I kind of figured," I grumble. The least I can do is play nice with his girlfriend. I just hope that he's serious about her before I try and become her friend. I love my brother, but his track record with women isn't that great.

Then again, neither was Tane's.

"He's serious about her. You don't have to be scared to get close to her," Levi states.

He knows me too well. "Yeah, alright."

"So. Sydney?" he prods.

"I'd like to surprise Tane. He's been messaging me all the time saying he's missing us, and calling every chance he can get."

"Well there you go then, book your ticket," he says. "You must be loaded with cash seeing as you're mortgage-free."

"You heard about that, huh?"

He laughs. "Oh, I heard about it. I wish I was there to see your face."

I roll my eyes. "I was surprised, happy, and kind of angry."

"I'll bet."

"Also grateful. It feels nice to have someone taking care of me, you know?" I admit.

"You deserve it." The sadness in his eyes makes me feel bad for talking to him about Tane and me.

"How's work going?" I ask, changing the subject.

"Really good, actually. Installed a bunch of systems this week. Crime rate is getting higher and higher, so the people who can afford the best security are asking for it," he says. "We've also installed some free-of-charge to a few schools and places like that."

I lower my brows. "You guys are so great. I'm so proud of you both."

"We're proud of you too, Giselle. Now go and book that ticket."

I nod. Looks like I'm going to surprise my man.

Chapter Twenty-three

Tane

Another gig comes to an end. I'm walking out of the club when I see a familiar face, but not a welcomed one. Maybe he didn't see me?

"Tane?"

Well, fuck.

I turn and muster a smile for Eddie, Keiran's best friend. He's the one who Keiran first started doing drugs with, long before I ever entered the scene.

"How have you been, bro?" he asks, looking me up and down.

"I've been okay," I reply in a careful tone, neither friendly nor rude "And yourself?"

He shrugs, and rubs his red eyes. "I miss him, you know?"

Of course I know.

"Yeah," I mumble, looking down. "I miss him too."

Every day.

"What are you doing here?" I ask. Last I heard he was in Eastern Europe doing God-knows-what.

"Just coming to see some mates," he says, itching his nose agitatedly. "Do you want to hang out for a bit? Reminisce a little? I hate it that I don't have anyone to talk about him with anymore."

I look around us.

"I have thirty minutes before I have to be somewhere," I lie.

He nods. "Cool, that's better than nothing. I know a place, a pub just across the road."

I swallow hard and follow him. Thirty minutes. That's it. I can do that.

*****

Giselle

Bag on my shoulder, I walk through the hotel and onto the seventh floor. Tane told me he was staying in room seven hundred and two, so that's what room I search for. I knock twice, then take a step back and wait for him to open the door. A couple of seconds pass before I see his face. Green eyes widen and his mouth drops open. I jump into his arms before his surprise can wear off.

"Giselle." He smiles down at me, eyes roaming over me greedily. "You just made my night."

My lips find his, showing him just how badly I'd missed him.

"I missed you," I say against his mouth. "I thought I'd surprise you. It was actually Levi's idea."

He raises his eyebrows. "Remind me to thank him."

He puts me down and locks the door. I throw my bag down in the corner and sit down on the bed, smiling widely. "How was your set?"

"Good. I saw an old friend afterwards, had a chat, then came back to the room," he says, not taking his eyes away from me.

He has that look in his eyes; the one that says he wants me badly.

"Do you want something?" I ask him, playing coy.

He kneels between my legs and kisses me gently. "You. Always you."

"Right answer," I whisper, smiling as he pulls my t-shirt off and throws it onto the floor.

"I can't believe you flew all the way here," he says, shaking his head as his eyes roam over my lace bra.

I shrug. "It's not like it's on the other side of the world."

"Parker …?"

"Is fine."

"So you can stay for the next two nights?" he asks, unclasping my white lace bra, pushing it down my arms and letting it fall.

"Yes," I pant as he sucks my left nipple into his mouth. He pulls my jeans off with my panties so that I'm sitting before him completely naked, while he's fully clothed.

"Oh yes," I moan, as he switches between my nipples, latching on and sucking hard. I wrap my legs around him and arch backwards, rubbing myself against him. His hand goes between my legs and he lets out a groan when he feels how wet I am. *Soaking.*

He pulls back, making me whimper, but when he pulls off his shirt my arguing stops. He stands up in front of me and drops his pants, stepping out of them. Looking up at him, I take his length into my hands, only to slide him into my mouth.

"Fuck," he moans, his hands knotting in my hair. "Fuck, yes!" I start pumping him in and out of my mouth and I can feel him getting closer. Suddenly he pulls away.

"Not yet." He pulls me up so I'm standing in front of him and kisses me deeply. Just as suddenly, he turns me around and gently guides me down onto the bed. Lying on my stomach, I anticipate what comes next.

He lies on top of my back, and I welcome his weight. He moves my hair to the side and kisses my neck as he guides his shaft inside me. I moan, pushing my ass back into him, wanting him to go faster. He grabs my hands and pulls them up towards the headboard, pinning me there.

"Patience," he tells me, and I can hear the smile in his voice. Slowly he rocks into me. He grips my hip with one of his hands and starts to speed up.

"Faster, Tane," I beg. He chuckles into my ear before he stops teasing and thrusts into me completely. I yell out, loving the feel of him deep inside me.

When his hand slips around my hip and rubs my clit, I explode. My moans turn to screams as I come hard. Tane follows me, and I feel him shudder against my body as he shoots inside me.

After gently sliding out he rolls over, no doubt not wanting to collapse on top of me. I turn towards him and kiss his shoulder.

"God I've missed you," he says, his eyes warm with love.

"I've missed you too, Tane," I say. I lean forward and kiss him, savouring his taste.

*****

Giselle

I walk into the bathroom to have a quick shower after our second round of lovemaking. I turn on the water and step in, letting it cascade over my body. When I'm done, I turn it off and jump out, grabbing two white fluffy towels from the shelf. I wrap one around my body, and one around my wet hair. Wiping the steam from the mirror, I'm about to start towel-drying my hair when I see something sitting next to the sink. I pick up the little bag, filled with a powdery white substance as dread fills me.

He wouldn't. Would he?

Why else would it be here?

My mind races.

My throat burns.

My heart breaks.

I open the door and walk out, staring at Tane lying there on the bed, a sated look on his handsome face.

"What is this?" I ask in a croaky voice.

He lifts his head up, looking at me, and then at the little bag in my hands.

His eyes widen and colour rises in his cheeks. "What the fuck …?"

My thoughts exactly.

"How could you do this, Tane?" I yell at him, my hands shaking. I grab my bag and walk back into the bathroom, locking the door behind me. I empty the drugs into the toilet and flush it, then throw the little bag in the trash. Then I get dressed and dry my hair as he knocks on the door, calling out my name, begging me to listen to him.

I block him out. How else could the drugs get here, in his room? There is only a little in the bag; did he use some? Or maybe he was going to?

Fuck.

I pack all my things up, and walk out of the bathroom. Tane is sitting on the bed, his head in his hands. "Giselle, please listen."

I look at him, not saying anything.

"I haven't … I wouldn't …"

I don't know what to say. I've heard that people on drugs lie. They lie to cover their tracks and they lie to get what they want. Would Tane lie?

Is this *my* Tane?

How much things have changed in the last hour. I went from being the happiest woman on the face of the earth to feeling so damn disappointed that I don't even know what to do with myself.

I have to get the hell out of here.

"I don't know what to think right now," I manage to get out.

Why, Tane?

"I wouldn't do this to you," he says. "I wouldn't."

Then why was it in your bathroom? I want to ask but I don't.

"I don't know where it came from," he says, cringing a little.

See? Even he knows it sounds bad. But he hasn't given me any indication that I'd have to worry about him.

"I don't know what to say to you right now," I admit to him. I don't know how to handle this. I have Parker to think about. If Tane is back on drugs, he will have to go back to rehab. *Parker will be devastated.*

Everything is so fucked up right now. My emotions are scattered, so I do the only thing I can think of. I walk away. "I need time to think, Tane. Can we talk about it when you get home?"

He looks down, but nods.

I leave, hearing a loud crash as I close the door. The sound makes me flinch, but I keep on walking. I need to think.

But I leave half of my heart with him.

*****

Tane

When she leaves, I don't stop her. Instead, I punch the wall. It leaves a dent in the plaster, and I don't give a shit.

How did this happen? How could I have been so stupid? When Eddie walked me back to my room, then asked if he could quickly use the bathroom, I didn't think anything of it. Clearly, I should have. Why did I trust him? He clearly hasn't changed and I should have followed my gut instinct and walked away from him. Yes, he did want to talk about old times with my cousin, and it was nice. I like hearing stories about Keiran. But the thing about Eddie is I guess he wants me to fail, to be like him. He's lonely and looking for a partner-in-crime. What else could it be?

I try and give him the benefit of the doubt. Maybe it was an accident. Maybe it slipped out of his pocket or something. Why else would he have left that cocaine in the bathroom? In my fucking room, when he knew I was clean.

I told him I was clean.

Fucking bastard.

I pace the hotel room. Why didn't she believe me? Of course it looked bad, but why didn't she give me a chance to explain myself? Did she expect me to fuck up? I walk into the bathroom and see the almost empty bag in the bin. I pick it up and examine it. I dip my finger into it and collect the small amount of remaining powder on my finger.

She thinks I did it. What difference would it make if I actually did? And such a small amount too.

It wouldn't even do anything. It would just be a tiny taste.

I flush the bag down the toilet. I turn on the tap and wash my hands. I'm better than this; I know I am.

Stronger.

I stare at myself in the mirror. My son needs me. My fiancée needs me. They're both counting on me. But more than that—I deserve better than this. I am better than this.

Nothing controls me anymore. I control my own actions.

I fought to be here, and I'll fight to stay. I won't let this selfish disease take control of me again. I deserve Giselle and Parker. Yes, I made some mistakes, but they are in the past, and there is no point looking back. I pack my suitcase.

Time for me to find Giselle and explain the truth. Make her listen.

Fuck work. I'd rather be at home with my family anyway.

I walk out of the room, more determined than I've ever been.

My soon-to-be wife better be ready to listen to what I have to say.

Chapter Twenty-four

Giselle

It takes me a while to hail a cab but when I do I jump in quickly, asking the driver to take me to the airport. A few silent tears drip down my cheeks, but I make no movement to dry them. Staring out the window, I wonder what would have happened if I hadn't shown up in his room. Would I ever have found out? I exhale heavily and cross my arms over my chest.

The drive goes quicker than I'd wished. I walk up to the service counter and book the next flight out, which happens to be departing in forty minutes, and boarding right now. Finally, some luck.

I think of making a call to Levi and Gage, but I don't want to talk about it right now. That would make it real.

I'm definitely not ready for that.

I will call someone when I land.

The lady hands me back my credit card and I accept the boarding pass and walk through security.

When I hear my name being called, I think I'm imagining it, but then I turn my head and see an angry looking Tane trying to walk towards me, but he's being held back by the airline security.

He's angry?

Why the hell is *he* angry?

He talks to the man, but the man shakes his head no.

They won't let him come after me.

When he calls out my name, my heart breaks further.

I turn and walk away and board the plane. Only when I sit down in my seat do I allow more tears to fall.

*****

I call my brother and tell him that I'm back in Perth. I tell him I'll catch a taxi to his house, but he says no, he or Levi will come now and get me, so I plop down in a chair in the Perth airport and wait for one of them to arrive. I put my phone on but ignore the countless number of missed calls and text messages from Tane. He and I need to have a talk. Me running away wasn't the best course of action, I know that, but I couldn't handle it. Maybe he didn't touch the drugs? Maybe he was only considering it? Maybe there is still a chance? He could talk to his sponsor. He told me about him one night, a man named Timothy.

Maybe I'm just so in love with him that I'm looking for excuses.

Great, I've become one of *those* women.

Fifteen minutes pass, then Levi walks up to me, a worried look on his face.

"What the hell happened?" he asks, scowling.

"I don't want to talk about it right now so please don't make me," I grumble as he carries my bag for me.

"Now I feel like shit. It was my idea that you went there."

"This was not your fault, Levi. You were being amazing, as usual," I tell him. "Thank you for coming to get me. I told Gage I was happy to jump in a taxi."

"Well, when you rang we were both worried, and Bianca was over, so I said I'd come and get you," he tells me, opening the car door for me.

"You're so good to me." I sigh, closing the door and putting my seat belt on.

Soft music plays on the radio as we drive home.

"You're going to have to tell us what happened," Levi says after some time.

"I will," I tell him, but don't say anything else. I'm almost embarrassed to admit what happened. How do I say, *I went into his bathroom and found drugs?* Just throw it out there?

"Are you trying to protect him?" Levi asks.

Is that what I was doing?

"I guess I just don't know what to do," I admit. If he did have to go back to rehab, would I stick by him, wait for him to come out and try again?

Yes, I would wait for him. I'd do anything for him. I'd want to be there for him and help him in any way I could.

Be his rock.

"I think I've messed up," I admit.

"Everyone makes mistakes, Giselle. Tane is a good man, and I know for a fact he's crazy about you. I'm happy for the two of you. Everyone knew you were meant to be together."

I shouldn't have left him. Why did I leave? I should have stayed there so we could talk it out. I should have trusted him. He hasn't given me a reason not to. I acted irrationally.

I ran.

Why did I run?

Tane needed me right then, and I bailed when I should have been there by his side, offering help.

What if he needs help?

I won't give up on him.

"You're right," I tell Levi. He's always right. "I love you. You know that, don't you?"

"Yes, I do, and the feeling is mutual. Now talk to me, Giselle," Levi says in a low tone.

I open my mouth to tell him everything, but suddenly the car jerks on the gravelly road.

"Shit," Levi says. The car swerves out of control and Levi pulls on the steering wheel, trying to correct its path. All it does it make the car go skidding the other way, so when he pulls on the wheel one more time, the car goes flying.

It happens so fast. I'm not sure how many times we rolled. It could be once. It could be five times. My head hits the roof and the window, causing sharp stabs of pain that turns into a relentless throbbing. The car finally stops moving and we're tilted on the side, my side down.

When my vision clears, I turn to look at Levi. His face is covered in blood but I can't identify the source. It's splattering onto me and my panic increases.

"Levi?" I croak. He doesn't respond. "LEVI!"

He doesn't even move.

I hear someone calling out to us but my vision goes blurry. A concerned man's face appears in my window and it's the last thing I see before everything goes black.

*****

I wake to my whole body hurting. I feel stiff. My eyes flutter open in confusion. Where was I?

"Gage?" I rasp when I see my brother flopped down in a chair near my bed. He lifts his head, eyes red and swollen. He looks like shit.

"How are you feeling?" he asks, standing and holding my hand.

His is ice-cold.

"What happened?" I ask him.

"You were in a car crash," he says hoarsely.

"Parker?"

"He's safe, don't worry. Do you remember what happened?" he asks in a careful tone.

Memories flash. The car rolling. Levi.

"Levi," I say, tears pooling in my eyes. "Where is he?"

I remember the last time I saw his face covered in blood.

Gage shakes his head and starts to cry. My brother. I've never seen him cry since we were children.

Instantly, I know. Nothing else would bring Gage to look this devastated.

"No," I say shaking my head, the brace around my neck restricting my movement. "No. No. No."

Gage covers his face with his hands. "He didn't make it, Giselle."

He didn't make it.

Four words.

He didn't make it.

Levi.

I shatter. My world crumbles. No, he can't be gone?

"No!" I wail, breaking down in hysterical sobs.

We cry together. We cry for all that we've lost.

We cry for Levi.

This is all my fault. He shouldn't have had to get up to pick me up from the airport. I should have taken in a taxi.

Why didn't I get in a taxi?

Gage scrubs his hand down his face. "This is all my fault."

Wait, what?

"I asked him to get you because I was with Bianca. It should have been me."

Guess I wasn't the only one blaming myself.

"It wasn't." It's all I manage to say. "Why did this happen?"

"Fuck Giselle, thank God you're alright," Gage mutters, leaning over me and kissing my brow. "If I lost you too …" He pauses. "I'll be back. Parker is in the waiting room with Bianca."

A nurse walks in, wanting to check me over.

Gage walks out and I'm left feeling empty. Destroyed. Like someone who just lost her best friend.

Chapter Twenty-five

Giselle

I'm kept in the hospital overnight. I'm fine, just a little bruised up. I had a concussion, so the doctors want to keep an eye on me. Parker and Gage spend the day with me, then go home at around six pm.

When Tane walks in an hour later, I'm surprised to see him. He rushes over to my bed, a big bouquet of flowers in his hands. He puts them on the table and turns to me, his eyes filled with worry and pain.

"I'm so sorry," he whispers, threading his fingers with mine. "God, I'm so sorry."

I stare into his eyes. "I can't believe he's gone."

He swallows and lowers his gaze. "I know."

"I shouldn't have run out on you; I should have stayed. Then Levi would still be alive."

"You can't think like that," he admonishes me gently.

"I know." But I can't seem to stop myself. There are so many *what if*s that are going to drive me crazy. So many factors that if they changed, could have made Levi still be alive right now.

And it kills me.

"How are you?" he asks, gently touching the scrape on my cheek.

"I'm okay." Physically, at least. "I can go home tomorrow."

I look at his rumpled clothes. "Did you come here straight from the airport?"

"Yes," he replies softly. "I went back and picked up my suitcase then had to wait for the next flight. Gage called me just as I was boarding the plane."

"I'm sorry," I say. Levi was his friend, too, not just mine.

He sighs sadly and cradles my face with his palms. "If anything had happened to you …"

"I'm okay. I'm alive …"

Which is more than I can say for Levi. Soon I'm crying again, this time in Tane's arms.

"Why do bad things happen to good people?" I sob into his chest.

"Shhh," he soothes, rubbing my back, kissing the top of my head.

He makes me feel like it's going to be okay, even though it isn't. Nothing can bring Levi back; nothing. How am I ever going to learn to live with that? To live without him?

*****

Two weeks later

I'm in bed watching *Friends* reruns when Tane walks in. He has a stubborn look on his face that I've seen before. He's been tiptoeing around me for the last two weeks, cooking for me, helping with everything that needs to be done. He's been amazing. Letting me sew myself together bit by bit, giving me time to heal.

Not pushing me.

But by the determined look on his face, that time is now over.

"I think it's time we spoke about what happened that night in the hotel room," he says.

Right, the huge elephant in the room. We still haven't spoken about what happened. After I left the hospital we had Levi's funeral to plan. Since his funeral, I pretty much haven't left my bed.

Tane's been taking Parker to and from kindy and doing everything for him. He's been keeping it all together, while I've been falling apart.

"I'm going to talk and you're going to listen," he says when I stay quiet.

I open my mouth, then close it. I'm surprised by his tone. He's never spoken to me like that.

Hard.

Unmoving.

He holds all my attention.

"I haven't taken any drugs," he starts. "I told you I ran into an old friend. He was Keiran's best friend." He pauses, making sure he has my attention. "He wanted to catch up, said he needed someone to talk to about Keiran. He misses him. So do I. We grabbed some food at the pub and chatted for a while, and it was good. I told him all about you and Parker, and how I'd been clean for more than a year now."

He looks at me with an intensity that makes me gulp. "Keep going," I say.

"Afterwards he walked me back to my room. I guess he was just lonely. He asked to use my bathroom and of course I let him. He must have left it there either accidentally or maybe as an attempt to tempt me."

"And were you tempted?" I ask. My stomach is clenching, I'm so nervous about his answer.

"I didn't even know it was there until you showed it to me. Do I ever get tempted? Of course. Those feelings won't just go away, Giselle. But all I think about are you and Parker, and I know that absolutely nothing is worth losing my family." He tentatively edges closer and takes me by the hands, kissing each one in turn. "I know it looks bad, but it's the truth. If I had messed up, I'd deserve your wrath, but that isn't the case at all," he says, staring straight ahead as he speaks.

"Why would your so-called friend do this to you?" I ask.

He sighs. "He was in even deeper than Keiran and me. I guess he wanted me back in that lifestyle with him. He must have been lonely and wanted a running partner. I don't know, I can only guess."

"Tane, look at me," I say.

He does. I search his familiar eyes and see no deceit. "You promise you're telling the truth?"

He holds my stare. "I promise."

"Okay," I say. "I believe you. I should have listened to you that night. I handled everything horribly, and I'm sorry."

He slowly nods. "When you said I needed to want to stay clean for me, not you and Parker, you were right. I deserve to be happy with the two of you. And I won't do anything to ruin that. I love you, Giselle, I always have."

I smile at that. "I know. You've always been mine."

He laughs. "Yes, I have."

"You can talk to me, you know, about anything. I want to be there for you, and I'm sorry that I haven't been."

He nods and smiles at me. "Okay. Now stop being stubborn and give me a kiss."

I do just that.

"We lost Levi," he says, "but you need to get up and out of this bed. Our son needs you. Justin needs you."

"I know," I tell him, tears filling my eyes. "It's just not fair."

"No, it's not," he agrees, voice breaking slightly.

He gives me his hand for me to stand up. I take it, squeezing his larger hand in mine.

I believe his words. I just hope that I'm right to trust my instincts on this one.

Trust.

Honesty.

Commitment.

I value these things, and I know Tane does too.

I trust him. And I will until he gives me a reason not to.

*****

Giselle

I answer the door wearing nothing but my ratty robe. When I see Bianca standing there, I do a double-take. "Ummm, hello."

"Hello Giselle," she says, smiling sweetly. "I brought you some cake, and I thought we could have a talk?"

I do like cake.

I open the door and let her in. I'm home alone and wasn't really expecting any company, but not much I can do about it now.

"I'm sorry about Levi," she starts, exhaling deeply as she sits down at my dining table. I nod and look down at the mention of him. "Gage isn't taking it so well. I'm trying to be there for him as much as I can. I'm just happy he hasn't completely shut me out."

"I'm glad my brother has you to be there for him," I manage to say.

"Well that's the thing. I was kind of hoping you would let me be there for you as well," she says.

I lift my head. "What do you mean?"

"I love your brother," she says. "And you're a big part of his life. I was hoping we could get to know each other. Be friends."

I smile. "That sounds great, Bianca."

"Maybe we could go out for dinner and drinks sometime next week?" she asks.

"Yeah, I could do that."

"Great," she replies, looking relieved.

"Now can I have some of that cake?"

She laughs. "So Gage was right then; bringing the cake was a good idea?"

I should have known my brother was behind this.

"Would you like some coffee?" I offer.

"I'd love some," she replies.

I get up and make her some, and we spend the rest of the morning chatting. Turns out Gage's taste in women isn't so bad after all.

*****

Gage and I sit side by side in the sand, letting the small waves wash over our feet.

"How are you?" I ask him, squinting against the sunlight.

"As can be expected. He was my brother, you know?"

"I do know," I whisper. It's been a month. It doesn't feel like it's getting easier, but we're trying to move forward.

"Do you know why Levi never entered any surfing comps? Why he didn't want to go pro?"

"No," I reply. I didn't know why. Levi had always told me he wasn't interested, that he loved surfing more than anything and he didn't need to go pro to do it. He told me he was happy with how things were.

"He didn't want to leave you and Parker," he says quietly. "He said he was happy staying here, in Perth."

I swallow hard, the pain in my chest tripling.

"Bianca has been amazing," he says so quietly I almost don't hear him.

"I know she has. You're lucky to have her," I say.

"Thank fuck you like her." He sighs.

I laugh. "I like anyone who makes you happy, Gage."

He turns to me, sunglasses covering his eyes. "Thanks, Giselle."

"You know, if you two have a kid I owe you a shitload of babysitting."

He laughs. "Fuck yeah you do."

"Thanks for always being there for me. I couldn't have asked for a better brother," I tell him, playing with the sand with my fingers.

He clears his throat. "You know I love you, baby sister."

"I do."

His actions always tell me so; he doesn't need to say the words.

"I'm going to surf for a bit," he says, going deeper into the water with Levi's board in his hand.

I watch him surf and imagine Levi is right there next to him.

*****

Tane

"Hello, Leanne Davies speaking," a female voice answers. I take a deep breath. This won't be easy.

"Hey Leanne, it's me, Tane." I don't have to wait long for the onslaught.

"Tane! What the hell is going on? You're supposed to be in New York in ten hours." She's pissed, and she has a right to be. Unfortunately, she's going to have to deal.

"Yeah, about that …" I begin. "I'm not going."

"You're not …" she says in confusion. "What the hell do you mean you're not going?"

"I don't want to do any more shows, Leanne."

"That's not my problem, Tane," she says. Her frustration is near palpable. "You entered into contracts.

You're legally obligated to be at these shows unless you have a damn good reason not to be."

"Call the promoters and tell them I'll return the money, with interest. Tell them it's a family emergency."

"Is it?" she asks. I swear she sounds concerned.

"Kind of," I say ambiguously. "I can't be away from my son and fiancée right now."

"So what do you want me to do?" she asks.

"Cancel the rest of the gigs I signed up for. I'm not going to perform any time soon, but I will still be producing, so keep the label updated."

"You owe me," is all she says as she hangs up. I breathe a sigh of relief. That woman scares me sometimes.

Now I can be with my family.

Epilogue

Tane

One year later

"And you may now kiss the bride," the pastor says.

I don't need to be told twice. I lift the veil off her beautiful face and lean down for a taste of her plump lips, sealing our fate. I lift her in the air, smiling against her lips at the cheers and catcalls.

Giselle Miller is now my wife.

And I couldn't be happier, or more in love.

I put her down, kissing her one last time before stepping away. I take her hand in mine, and face the crowd. Parker runs to our side. Dressed in a suit, he looks like the miniature version of me.

My little family.

I'm so proud of them, so happy to be with them every day. There is nowhere else in the world I would want to be.

I look at the woman standing beside me. I flash back to her at three, poking her tongue out at me. Then her at eight, chasing after us as Gage and I were playing. I see her at eleven, beating us at video games. Her at fourteen, trying to kiss me, and me refusing because she was too young—no matter how much I just wanted a taste. Her at sixteen, her face full of grief just before I left her. Me finally kissing her. Mouthing to her that I love her.

Now here she is, smiling widely, happy to be my wife. She's always been in my life, and she always will be.

We walk on the sand through the middle of the crowd, thanking everyone for their wishes and attendance today.

"Are you ready, husband?" she asks as a few people start to head to the reception.

"I've always been ready," I reply, unable to stop myself from one last kiss. I then lift Parker up on my shoulders.

We walk together. I wish my mother were here; I know she'd be so happy. She always loved Giselle.

I put Parker down and look at the sky for a second, thinking of her. Wrapping my arm around my wife, I kiss the top of her strawberry-scented hair.

"I love you," I tell her. "More than words can express."

"I love you too," she breathes back.

I can't wait to see what she's wearing underneath her dress.

She raises an eyebrow. "Let's get this reception over with."

I grin down at her. "Let's."

*****

Giselle

I plop down next to Levi's headstone and place the flowers.

"You didn't even like flowers," I mumble. "But I don't like your headstone looking bare."

I sigh and put my hand on the letters of his name engraved into the marble. "I miss you. Every damn day, Levi. I still see Justin every week, and I made sure that all your money will go to him when he turns eighteen. He will want for nothing."

Without Levi there to help her, Keira has put aside everything and lets us see Justin.

I retract my hand and pull out the crumbled photo of Levi, Parker, Justin and me. "Parker misses you. We go surfing in your spot and think of you. Well, they surf, and I swim," I correct. "We talk about you all the time."

I stand up and place the photo down next to the flowers. "I'll never forget you, Levi. I'll see you same time next week."

I turn around and walk to my car. I see Gage's car pull into the cemetery car park, and I wave at him.

He slides out with Bianca, who is now his wife. I love her almost as much as Gage does.

I watch as the two of them place down their own flowers, tears flowing when Gage gets down on his knees and rests his head on the headstone.

You were loved, Levi; you were loved.

The End

About the Author

New York Times & USA Today Bestselling Author Chantal Fernando is twenty six years old and lives in Western Australia.

When not reading, writing or daydreaming she can be found enjoying life with her three sons and family.

Chantal loves to hear from readers and can be found on her [FB author page](#) or her [website](#).

Made in the USA
Middletown, DE
17 January 2016